D.

"May we help you?" Frank asked the two men

The older of the two stared at Frank, then turned his gaze to Ziggy and Petra. "Yes, you can."

Then, like a snake uncoiling to strike, the man pulled a small blackjack from his pocket and struck Joe on the chin. Joe staggered to the side, slamming into Frank, and both of them lost their balance and fell to the ground.

The younger man grabbed Petra and pulled her into the alley.

"Hey!" Ziggy yelled, and burst into the alley. Frank and Joe jumped up and followed him.

A bright glint of steel drew Joe's attention to the man who held Petra. Joe saw that one hand covered her mouth and the other held a switchblade to her throat.

Joe started toward the younger man.

"Don't try it, mate," the older man growled from behind him, "or we'll kill the girl."

Books in THE HARDY BOYS CASEFILES® Series

#1 DEAD ON TARGET
#2 EVIL, INC.
#3 CULT OF CRIME
#4 THE LAZARUS PLOT
#5 EDGE OF DESTRUCTION
#6 THE CROWNING TERROR
#7 DEATHGAME
#8 SEE NO EVIL
#9 THE GENIUS THIEVES
#10 HOSTAGES OF HATE
#11 BROTHER AGAINST BROTHER
#12 PERFECT GETAWAY
#13 THE BORGIA DAGGER
#14 TOO MANY TRAITORS
#15 BLOOD RELATIONS
#16 LINE OF FIRE
#17 THE NUMBER FILE
#18 A KILLING IN THE MARKET
#19 NIGHTMARE IN ANGEL CITY
#20 WITNESS TO MURDER
#21 STREET SPIES

#22 DOUBLE EXPOSURE
#23 DISASTER FOR HIRE
#24 SCENE OF THE CRIME
#25 THE BORDERLINE CASE
#26 TROUBLE IN THE PIPELINE
#27 NOWHERE TO RUN
#28 COUNTDOWN TO TERROR
#29 THICK AS THIEVES
#30 THE DEADLIEST DARE
#31 WITHOUT A TRACE
#32 BLOOD MONEY
#33 COLLISION COURSE
#34 FINAL CUT
#35 THE DEAD SEASON
#36 RUNNING ON EMPTY
#37 DANGER ZONE
#38 DIPLOMATIC DECEIT
#39 FLESH AND BLOOD
#40 FRIGHT WAVE
#41 HIGHWAY ROBBERY
#42 THE LAST LAUGH
#43 STRATEGIC MOVES

Available from ARCHWAY Paperbacks

THE HARDY BOYS CASEFILES NO. 43

STRATEGIC MOVES

FRANKLIN W. DIXON

AN ARCHWAY PAPERBACK
Published by POCKET BOOKS
New York   London   Toronto   Sydney   Tokyo   Singapore

AN ARCHWAY PAPERBACK *Original*

 An Archway Paperback published by
POCKET BOOKS, a division of Simon & Schuster Inc.
1230 Avenue of the Americas, New York, NY 10020

ISBN: 0-671-70040-5

First Archway Paperback printing September 1990

10 9 8 7 6 5 4 3 2 1

THE HARDY BOYS, AN ARCHWAY PAPERBACK
and colophon are registered trademarks of Simon & Schuster Inc.

THE HARDY BOYS CASEFILES is a trademark
of Simon & Schuster Inc.

Printed in U.S.A.

IL 7+

Chapter

1

"ARE YOU SURE we haven't driven into the Twilight Zone and been zapped back to Shakespeare's time?" Joe Hardy sat on the edge of the car's backseat, peering into the distance, his blue eyes wide; beneath his blond hair his forehead was wrinkled in confusion.

"Quite sure, guv," the driver answered with a chuckle and a clipped British accent. Davey Bolan, in his early twenties, short, dark-haired, and friendly, shifted into low gear as the small black British car topped a low hill.

Frank Hardy, at eighteen, a year older than Joe, sat next to his brother, the draft from the window blowing back his brown hair. "Joe has a limited view of other countries, Davey," he announced.

1

Joe frowned at Frank and then turned to look back down the road. They were nearing Oxford, England, and Joe's attention had been attracted by the ancient needle-pointed spires that threaded the blue English sky and the Gothic turrets and pinnacles of the churches that were silhouetted against white rolling clouds.

Three months earlier the Hardys had received a special invitation to attend the International Classroom, a new program sponsored by the University of Oxford. The best and brightest high school students from several countries had been invited to spend two weeks at Oxford, England's oldest university.

Fenton Hardy, the internationally known private detective, had agreed to let his sons attend, but only after they had promised to stay out of trouble. The brothers had enthusiastically agreed, but Frank could tell by his father's troubled look that the older Hardy was worried nonetheless.

Davey, an employee of the university, had met them at Heathrow Airport, outside London. The Hardys were the last of some one hundred students to arrive; most had come the day before, Saturday.

Frank looked out a window as they crossed a bridge and entered Oxford proper. The outlying neighborhoods had appeared modern, with neat rows of houses. But after crossing the bridge, Frank felt as though they had indeed gone through a time warp. The street had narrowed and was paved with bricks. The car rattled as it made its way over the unevenly worn surface. And the buildings looked several centuries older than the ones on the outskirts of town.

"That's Maudlin College on the right." Davey pointed with his thumb. "Those spires you were looking at on the hilltop, Mr. Hardy, belong to the cloisters of Bell Tower and Founder's Tower, two of the oldest. The colleges that make up Oxford University are spread throughout the town."

"I thought it was Magdalen College," Frank said.

"It's spelled 'Magdalen,' sir, but it's pronounced 'Maudlin,' " Davey replied. "No one really knows why."

"Probably for the same reason that the English say 'Tems' River instead of 'Thames,' the way it's spelled," Joe said. "Where's Brasenose, where we're staying?"

"Center of town on the High," Davey answered.

"The High?" Joe asked.

"All the streets are called by their nicknames," Frank replied. "Broad Street is simply the Broad; Cornmarket Street is the Corn; Bear Lane is the Bear. You should have spent more time reading the brochure instead of telling Chet Morton about how you were going to impress the English girls."

Davey laughed.

Joe nudged Frank with his elbow. "Very funny."

"Here we are, gents." Davey smoothly braked the car in front of an ancient-looking building, its bricks dark and old.

Frank and Joe stepped from the car. The sun was beginning to set, and a slight September chill filled the air. The brothers walked around to the back of the car and began helping Davey pull their suitcases from the trunk. Then the Hardys stared at the building.

"Brasenose College," Frank said in a tour guide's voice. "Founded 1509 and named for an ancient bronze nose-shaped knocker that once hung on its door."

"You'd make a great guidebook," Joe quipped.

Davey looked at his watch, then pointed toward the large wooden doors of Brasenose College. "You'll find your room assignments on the bulletin board inside—through those doors, down the corridor, then first hall on your left." He hopped back into the car. "I hope your stay in England is a pleasant and peaceful one." Davey waved and sped away from the Hardys.

Frank opened the heavy wooden door and ushered his brother inside Brasenose College.

They each took a sheet of paper off the bulletin board. The papers told them their room assignments and that dinner would be served in the Brasenose dining hall promptly at 6:30 P.M. Joe hadn't eaten anything since the meal on the airplane, and that had had all the flavor and consistency of plastic.

Their rooms were on the second floor of a dormitory a few yards from the main college. Joe liked the idea that the dorm was coed, with the female exchange students in the opposite wing.

"Each of the thirty-five colleges and five private halls is self-governing," Frank explained to Joe as they walked over to their dormitory, "with its own teachers, dorms, classrooms, and dining halls."

In a few minutes, Frank and Joe were standing in front of what would be home for the next two weeks. Like everything else they had noticed about Oxford, the dormitory looked old. Joe looked toward the top of the four-story building, where several large stone gargoyles stared down at them as though the two teenagers were the creatures' next meal. A shudder ran through Joe's body. He opened the large wooden doors, and he and Frank walked inside the ancient building.

"Here we are," Frank said after they had hauled their luggage up two flights of stairs. "You're just across the hall, in two-ten."

Frank knocked on the door of the room to which he had been assigned—two-eleven, across from Joe. Each exchange student was assigned a roommate from another country. The directors of the special two-week program were hoping that by living and working together the students would form new friendships.

"Come on in, partner," someone answered from inside in a poor imitation of a cowboy, his accent thick and heavy.

Joe smiled at Frank's puzzled expression. "Sounds like a real winner," he said as he knocked on the door of his room.

Frank only shrugged and pushed open the door.

Standing by a twin bed, putting shirts on a hanger, was a young man dressed in blue jeans, a blue western-cut shirt, and red cowboy boots.

"Hi," Frank said, and threw his suitcase onto the other twin bed. "I'm Frank Hardy, Bayport, USA."

The young man stuck out his hand. "Pyotr Zigonev, Kiev, USSR. Ziggy to my friends."

Frank grabbed the young man's hand. "Pleasure."

Frank sized up Ziggy: eighteen or nineteen, same height as Frank—six feet one—slight build, dark blond hair, blue eyes, intelligent-looking, and friendly. The only odd thing about the young man was that he was dressed more like an American square dancer than a Russian teenager.

Then Frank's eyes lit up. "Pyotr Zigonev? The Soviet junior chess champion?"

Pyotr blushed. "Yes. But call me Ziggy." He paused and then looked puzzled. "You know about me?"

"Know about you?" Frank was excited. "Next to computers, chess is my main interest."

"Not girls?" Ziggy's face showed confusion. "I thought all American boys were interested in girls."

"We are—I mean, I am," Frank said with a laugh.

The door opened and Joe walked in. "Hey, Frank, are we going to eat in the dining hall or in town?"

"Joe, this is Pyotr Zigonev," Frank said. "Pyotr, this is my brother, Joe."

"Ziggy," Ziggy said.

"Joe Hardy," Joe said, shaking the young man's hand. He turned to Frank. "So where are we eating?"

"Did you hear me? *Pyotr Zigonev.*"

Joe scowled. "I'm hungry, not deaf. Are we going to eat in town or at the dining hall?"

"Ziggy is the Soviet junior chess champion," Frank explained with exasperation.

"Congratulations," Joe said to Ziggy with a nod of his head, trying not to sound rude or impatient.

Frank frowned at Joe's apparent indifference. "That's like being the MVP of the Super Bowl and World Series in the same year," Frank blurted.

"The *what?*" Ziggy asked, confused.

Joe was becoming increasingly frustrated with

Frank. "That's great. I'm happy for him. But where are we going to eat?" he insisted.

"Let's eat off campus," came a soft accented voice from the doorway.

Joe turned around at the sound of the voice. His blue eyes widened, and he had to keep his jaw from dropping.

Joe's eyes were locked on a beautiful young woman. She stood several inches shorter than Joe and wore a dark blue blouse neatly tucked into a tight-fitting black leather miniskirt, both of which showed her to have a good figure. Her eyes were a velvety bright blue and drew Joe to them. Her hair was blond and cut short to reveal a soft white neck. Joe felt the blood rush to his feet.

Ziggy moved to the doorway. "This is my twin sister, Petra."

"Hi," Frank said. "I'm Frank Hardy, Bayport, USA." Frank shook Petra's hand.

"It is my pleasure," Petra said softly, her Russian accent sending goose bumps rushing up and down Joe's arms.

Joe took a deep breath and stretched to his full six-foot height. "Joe Hardy," he said, shaking Petra's hand.

"Twins also?" Petra flashed a shy smile at Joe.

Joe's mind raced as he tried to think of something clever and witty to say, but for the first time in his life a pretty girl had made him forget all his best one-liners. So he simply said, "No. Just brothers."

"I think Petra has a good idea," Ziggy said. "Tonight is the last night we can dress casually."

"What?" Joe asked, trying not to stare at Petra.

"You should have read the brochure," Frank whispered.

Petra continued to smile at Joe. "Tomorrow we must wear regulation clothes to class. Gentlemen: slacks, jackets, and school ties. Ladies: conservative blouses and mid-length skirts."

"Oh, yeah," Joe said knowingly. Too bad, Joe thought as he tried to keep from glancing down at Petra's legs. "I think your idea is great." He turned to Frank. "Let's eat out."

"Good idea, brother," Frank said with a grin.

They left the room, and a moment later the foursome stepped out of the dormitory and into an English twilight.

"I forgot my map of the city," Joe announced with a snap of his fingers. He started to go back inside.

"Never mind," Frank said. "I studied the map on the plane. We can find a pub if we go west on the High."

"You have a good memory," Petra cooed.

"A mind like a steel trap," Joe said, trying to make the remark sound like a joke. "And about as interesting."

Ziggy laughed. "I love American humor."

"I bet you can't wait to hear some," Frank said with a teasing smile at Joe.

"Let's go," Joe said, ignoring Frank. Joe was suddenly jolted backward as he bumped into a man who had stepped around the corner of the dormitory building.

"You are going nowhere," the man ordered. He unbuttoned his jacket and put his hands on his hips.

Joe was about to say something when he noticed the butt of an automatic pistol peeking out from the man's shoulder holster.

Chapter

2

"ALEKSANDR!" Petra said angrily.

"Who is this?" Frank asked.

"Aleksandr Dancek," Ziggy answered. "Our chaperon."

"Chaperon?" Joe was disappointed.

"Yes," Petra said. "The only way Mother and Father would approve our coming to Oxford was if we agreed to have a chaperon from the Soviet embassy in London."

"It is our bad luck to get someone who takes his job seriously," Ziggy said, smiling at Aleksandr.

"Where are you going?" Aleksandr demanded to know, ignoring Ziggy's jab.

"Leave the children alone," a woman said as she joined the group.

"Hello, Katrina," Petra said.

"It's getting a bit crowded," Joe observed.

"This is Katrina, Aleksandr's wife," Petra said.

"Hello," Katrina said, holding out her hand to Frank. She and Aleksandr looked to be in their late twenties. While Aleksandr had sharp, angular features and short-cropped black hair, Katrina was all smiles, soft-featured, blond, and friendly.

Frank introduced himself and then Joe. Aleksandr did not offer to shake hands.

"We were only going out to eat," Ziggy said.

"You are supposed to check with us first." Aleksandr's voice was stern, angry.

"You were not around," Ziggy replied.

"I think they will be okay, Alek," Katrina said.

"They are supposed to check with us first," Aleksandr repeated with a quick look of anger at Katrina. "Where do you plan to eat?" he asked Ziggy.

"We haven't decided," Ziggy replied. "We were just going to walk around with our new friends and find a pub."

Aleksandr sized up Frank and Joe, looking unimpressed. "You will be back by nine o'clock." It was an order, not a suggestion.

"We will be back when we are finished," Petra countered. "You are to be our chaperons and not our jailers. I would not want to write home to Father and tell him that you are making our stay in England an unpleasant one."

Aleksandr bristled.

Joe was surprised and impressed with the strong tone in Petra's voice and her determination not to be pushed around by the diplomat.

Aleksandr shifted nervously and buttoned up his jacket. "Ten o'clock. No later. You must get plenty of rest for your classes tomorrow."

"That is more reasonable," Petra replied.

"Come, Alek," Katrina said, sliding a hand through one of Aleksandr's arms. "Let's take a walk."

"I have work to do," Aleksandr said without emotion. He walked away from the group and entered the dorm.

"I suppose I will read a book," Katrina said. "You kids have fun." Then she, too, disappeared into the dormitory.

They had walked several yards before anybody said anything.

"Aleksandr has all the charm of a snake," Frank commented.

"He takes his job very seriously," Ziggy said.

"Seriously enough to carry a gun?" Joe asked.

"Gun?" Petra's voice showed surprise.

"I saw the butt of a gun when he opened his jacket."

"Are you sure?" Ziggy asked.

"I saw it, too," Frank said.

"Maybe you are mistaken," Ziggy said. "It is getting dark."

Frank glanced at Ziggy. It was obvious that neither Ziggy nor Petra wanted to talk about Aleksandr's gun. Frank let the subject drop—for the moment.

They turned west on the High and kept walking, Frank next to Ziggy, Joe next to Petra.

The streetlights flickered on as the evening made the transition from twilight to night.

The High was one of the oldest streets in Oxford as well as its main thoroughfare. Frank pointed out the twin ruts left in the brick road by the countless carriages, wagons, and coaches that had rumbled along its ancient course through the years.

Joe smiled at Petra. "How did you learn to speak English so well?"

"Mother is an English language instructor at the University of Kiev," Ziggy explained. "We practically grew up speaking your language."

Joe was a little annoyed. He had asked Petra, not Ziggy.

"Ziggy is a fanatic about American culture," Petra laughed. "That's why he wears those silly western clothes and tries to talk like John Wayne."

"These are not silly," Ziggy replied defensively.

"Actually," Frank began, "Ziggy would be right at home in Oklahoma or New Mexico."

"I am very much interested in cowboy movies,

especially John Wayne movies." Ziggy straightened up and in his best John Wayne voice, with a thick Russian accent, said, "Well, pilgrims, I'd say you better get on your horse and hightail it out of here before I kill ya—or worse!"

"Very good," Frank said, clapping.

Ziggy blushed. "Thanks, partner."

"What does your father do?" Frank asked, changing the subject.

Ziggy and Petra glanced at each other. Frank noticed that Ziggy raised his eyebrows in a silent question, and then Petra shook her head so slightly that the movement was barely noticeable.

Ziggy smiled and looked at Frank. "He works for the telephone company." Ziggy started walking next to his sister, almost shoving Joe out of the way.

Joe looked annoyed but remained uncharacteristically silent. He wanted to make a good impression on Petra, and getting angry at Ziggy wouldn't have helped.

Joe took a deep breath and looked at the mix of modern and ancient buildings along the High. The sidewalks were busy with people out for the evening.

Ziggy continued to talk about western movies while Petra pointed out the various shops she wanted to visit later in the week.

Frank couldn't shake the feeling that Ziggy and Petra had lied about their father and then changed the subject. He also did not believe their innocent act concerning Aleksandr's gun. Young junior diplomats did not carry weapons, especially in a foreign country. In fact, the only people who went about armed in a foreign country were secret agents. And why had Aleksandr looked worried and nervous when Petra mentioned that she would write to her father?

They walked several blocks before Joe, who was in the lead, stopped in front of a pub.

The building that housed the pub looked hundreds of years old and was in the Tudor style, with whitewashed stucco and heavy gray wooden beams. The windows were large and covered with a crisscross wooden lattice. Plants hung in the window, and a large sign over the door identified it as the Red Bull pub.

"This looks like a good place," Joe announced.

"It looks friendly enough," Petra said.

"If it serves food," Frank said, "it's a friend of Joe's."

Ziggy laughed.

Joe frowned at Frank and held the door open, letting Ziggy and Petra in, but stepping in front of Frank and nudging him back.

Frank held the door open, smiled, and followed Joe. Frank looked around the pub. The smell of smoke, grease, and furniture oil permeated the air. The highly polished oak walls were bare except for a Union Jack and a picture of Queen Elizabeth II. On a back wall, Frank saw a well-punctured dart board.

Noise from the tables floated in the air as thick as the pipe and cigarette smoke and became one constant drone.

They found a table in the corner by the window and ordered.

"What does your father do for the telephone company?" Frank asked. He was trying not to press the issue, afraid of scaring off Ziggy and Petra, but Ziggy's remark had sparked Frank's interest. So had Aleksandr's gun—and Aleksandr's apparent fear of Ziggy's father.

Again Ziggy and Petra exchanged glances.

"He is an administrator," Ziggy answered.

"And what does *your* father do?" Petra countered.

"He's a private detective," Joe answered. "So are we."

"You are too young to be detectives," Petra declared. "You are the same age as Ziggy and I."

"We help our father on cases from time to time," Frank said.

"We even work on our own cases," Joe added. "We have a pretty good track record."

"So you are in sports, too?" Ziggy asked seriously.

Joe frowned at Ziggy. "What?"

Frank laughed. " 'Track record' is an American expression. It means we've had success."

Joe ordered a hamburger, and the others chose Welsh rabbit. The new friends ate slowly

17

as they exchanged small talk about the differences and similarities in schools, boys and girls, parents, and everything else. Everything except the Zigonevs' father.

They left the pub an hour and a half later and headed back to Brasenose. The streets were all but deserted. They had begun to cross an alley when a voice stopped them.

"Excuse me," said a man just inside the alley.

The group stopped and turned. Frank looked at the two men who faced the four teenagers. The older man was short and stocky, his unshaven face flecked with gray and black stubble. The large bags beneath his eyes gave him a tired and haggard appearance. The cap he was wearing made his head look flat.

The other man was a couple of inches taller and was also thinner and younger than the first. He seemed nervous, always looking behind him or out into the street.

"May we help you?" Frank asked. The two men didn't look trustworthy to Frank. And the younger man's twitching bothered him.

The older man stared at Frank, then turned his gaze to Ziggy and Petra. After a moment he said, "Yes, you can."

Then, like a snake uncoiling to strike, the older man pulled a small blackjack from his pocket and struck Joe on the chin. Joe staggered to one side, slamming into Frank. Both of them lost their balance and fell to the ground.

The younger man grabbed Petra and pulled her into the alley.

"Hey!" Ziggy yelled, and burst into the alley. Frank and Joe jumped up and followed him.

The alley was lighted by a lone light bulb, creating harsh shadows that fell on the walls and ground. A bright glint of steel drew Joe's attention to the younger man, who held Petra. Joe saw that one hand covered her mouth and the other held a switchblade to her throat. Ziggy lay on the ground at the feet of the older man—unmoving.

Joe started toward the younger man.

"Don't try it, mate," the older man growled, "or we'll kill the girl."

Chapter

3

"WHAT DO YOU WANT?" Frank asked. "Money?" He reached behind him and began pulling his wallet out.

The younger man holding Petra tightened his grip.

"No funny business," the older man warned. "We don't want your stinking money, Yank."

Joe's blue eyes closed to angry slits. He stared at the younger man. "You've got five seconds to let her go or lose that arm."

The younger man glanced nervously at the older man.

"Impertinent young pup," the older man spit out. "We don't care about the girl. We only want the boy."

"What did you do to him?" Frank asked as he stood over his injured friend.

The older man smacked the blackjack against his hand. "You figure it out." He nudged Ziggy's side with the toe of a grimy boot. "Get up!"

Ziggy groaned and rolled over.

When the younger man looked down at Ziggy, Joe took advantage of the distraction and lunged at him and Petra. With his left hand he gripped the man's knife hand like a vise and twisted the knife away from Petra's throat. Joe then placed a well-aimed right jab squarely in the man's face, his fist breezing past Petra.

The man groaned and staggered back. Joe grabbed Petra and pulled her away from him.

He turned back to the younger man, who held up the knife. Joe could tell by the panic in his eyes and the fear on his face that he didn't want to tangle with Joe. Joe swung his right leg forward and kicked the knife out of the man's hand. Without hesitation, the man spun around and ran down the alley.

"Sammy!" the older man yelled. He turned and followed his partner through the alley, away from the Hardys.

Frank, who was tending to Petra and Ziggy, started to chase the older man. But the man was near the end of the alley and soon disappeared down a side street.

"Is everyone okay?" Frank asked the group.

"Yes," Petra gasped. "Thank you."

Frank could tell by the short, raspy breaths Petra was taking that she was shaken up by the incident.

"Why didn't you go after him?" Joe asked.

"I thought I'd better make sure that Ziggy was okay," Frank answered.

"Let's form a posse and hunt them down," Ziggy suggested.

"They're long gone by now, cowboy," Frank replied. He smiled at the disappointed look on Ziggy's face. He had known Ziggy for only a short time, but the young Russian was already a friend. "Looks as if you and Joe are going to have twin tattoos."

"What?" Ziggy asked.

"The bruises from the blackjack," Joe explained, rubbing his own swollen chin.

"Thanks for helping," Ziggy said. "We owe you one."

"Wh-what did they want?" Petra asked, a tremble in her voice.

"They wanted Ziggy," Frank said.

"Why?" Tears had welled up in Petra's eyes, and Joe could tell that she was fighting to hold them back.

"That's what we'd like to know," Joe said.

"Shouldn't we call the police?" Petra asked.

"Are you sure you want to do that?" Frank countered.

"What do you mean?" Ziggy asked.

"That older thug said he wanted Ziggy, not you, Petra," Frank said, glancing at Petra. "I interpret that to mean he wanted to kidnap Ziggy."

"Kidnap Ziggy? Why?" Petra's voice was controlled, but Joe saw fear in her blue eyes.

"That's what we want to find out," Frank said, his voice hard and serious. "But first, let's get out of this alley. There's a small fish-and-chips stand up the street."

They left the alley, Frank being the last out. Across the street a car pulled out of an alley, its lights striking Frank. It turned and sped past the four of them. Although partially blinded by the lights' glare, Frank had seen three men in the car, one driving, two in back. He had recognized two of them. The driver was Aleksandr Dancek. Frank also knew the second man, who had a round, plump face and wore a nondescript gray suit. The third man, a stranger, was on the opposite side of the car in the shadows, but Frank could see that he was large with sharp, chiseled features.

They reached the fish-and-chips stand, and Joe ordered four colas. Frank found a table away from the few customers sitting at the tables outside the stand.

"You are joking about those two desperadoes trying to kidnap us," Ziggy said after Joe had joined the group.

Frank didn't know if he could get used to hearing American cowboy slang spoken with a Russian accent by one of the world's foremost chess players.

He smiled at Ziggy to try to ease the tension. "Perhaps you can start by telling us about your father," Frank suggested.

"Why do you believe this involves our father?" Petra asked, her expression cold.

"We're detectives," Joe reminded her. "We make it a habit to study people, to understand their motives. You and Ziggy have avoided talking about your father."

"You have a choice," Frank added. "You can continue to hide the truth from us, or you can let us help you. You wanted to pay us back somehow for helping you in the alley. As Ziggy might say, we're calling in your IOUs now."

Petra looked down at her soft drink, avoiding Frank's eyes. Then she looked at Ziggy, who only stared at the table.

"Ziggy?" Petra asked softly.

Ziggy looked up. He smiled. "I believe we can trust the Hardys."

Petra spoke. "Our father is an engineer. He is with the communications section of a national security agency."

"KGB," Frank said.

Petra looked stunned at Frank's comment.

"Yes," Ziggy said. "But he is more of an administrator than a spy."

"It makes sense," Joe said. "Kidnapping the

son and daughter of a KGB official would almost ensure that the kidnappers would get whatever they want."

"No," Frank corrected. "They didn't want Petra."

"Why not?" Joe asked.

"Ziggy has two things going for him that would attract kidnappers." Frank drank some of his cola. "The first is that his father is in the KGB. The second is that Ziggy is a national hero to the people of the Soviet Union."

"Oh, I see," Joe replied, understanding Frank's point.

Frank was tempted to tell the others about the men in the car, but decided to wait and tell Joe in private. Two questions occurred to him: Did the men in the car see the attempted kidnapping? And if they did, why didn't they stop it?

They left the fish-and-chips stand and walked silently back to the dormitory, first escorting Petra to her room.

They met Katrina on the stairs. She had come to check on Petra. Frank asked about Aleksandr, and Katrina replied that he was asleep.

Why was Katrina lying? Frank wondered.

"I am tired," Ziggy said as they neared their rooms. "I will hit the hay."

"I'll be in in a minute," Frank said as Ziggy unlocked the door to their dorm room. "I want to talk to Joe."

" 'Night, cowpokes," Ziggy said, and shut the door.

"Quite a character," Frank said with a laugh.

"You know," Joe said, "I thought I'd get a roommate from France or Poland or Japan. Instead, I get a skateboarder from California." He leaned against the wall. "So, what do you think?

Frank knew what Joe meant. "I think we've got more than a simple kidnapping attempt."

"Evidence?"

Frank shook his head. "No. Just a hunch. Guess who I saw as we left the alley."

"Prince Charles?"

"I wouldn't have been surprised to see him," Frank said with a smile. "I saw Aleksandr Dancek driving a light blue British Ford sedan."

"Out for an evening drive," Joe replied.

"Katrina just said he was asleep."

Joe raised his eyebrows. "That's right."

"That's not all. What would Aleksandr, a Russian diplomat, be doing with the director of the Network?"

Joe pushed away from the wall. "What is the Gray Man doing in England?"

Joe knew as well as Frank that the Gray Man could be anywhere at any time doing anything that his duties required of him. As a member of the covert agency known as the Network, the Gray Man was primarily responsible for stopping terrorists before they acted on their mad impulses.

"The Assassins." Joe's voice was as hard as iron.

The Hardys had first met the Gray Man after Joe's girlfriend, Iola Morton, had been killed in a car bomb explosion. Since then, the Hardys, the Gray Man, and the Network had teamed up more than once to stop a deadly terrorist group known as the Assassins whenever they tried to bring chaos and murder to the world.

"I'm not so sure that terrorists are involved." Frank chose his words carefully after turning them over in his mind. "Aleksandr, the Gray Man, and one other character were parked in the alley across from where the four of us were attacked."

"And they didn't do anything to help," Joe added.

Frank didn't like what he was about to say, but he had to say it. "Perhaps they didn't do anything to help because they wanted Ziggy to be kidnapped."

Chapter

4

"WHY WOULD Aleksandr be involved?" Frank said, more to himself than to Joe.

Frank yawned and rubbed his eyes. It was almost eleven, and although he had slept on the plane from New York to London, the five-hour time difference was catching up with him.

"A double agent," Joe replied.

"He wouldn't risk being seen with the head of the Network." Frank yawned again.

"I suppose you're right," Joe said with a yawn. "Who do you think the other man was?"

"A Network agent," Frank replied.

"Or KGB."

Frank thrust his hands into his pockets. "This is getting deep."

"Let's keep our guard up." Joe unlocked the

door to his room. "Whoever is behind this didn't expect to fail the first time, and they're going to come out swinging."

"But we'll be ready for them the next time," Frank said, although he wasn't comforted by the thought that there would be a next time.

Joe stepped into his room and shut the door.

Frank stepped across the hallway to his room and put his hand on the doorknob.

The two who attacked Petra and Ziggy couldn't have been international terrorists, Frank thought. They acted and talked more like common criminals. Terrorists would have used deadlier means than a blackjack and a switchblade. Terrorists would not have left without their prey, even if it had meant spilling blood.

A thump diverted Frank's attention to the closed door to the left of his and Ziggy's room. In the crack beneath the door Frank could see the shadows of someone's feet. The person was standing just inside the door. Then the light in the room suddenly went off.

Frank crept to the door, held his breath, and pressed his ear against it. He could hear someone breathing on the other side.

He moved back from the door, tiptoed to his room, and went in. Ziggy was asleep, so Frank left the light off. In the darkness he found the one desk in the room. He pulled his penlight from his pocket and flipped it on. He shuffled through a sheaf of papers and found the room assignment list of the international students. Whoever was next door had been listening to Frank and Joe's conversation.

Frank wasn't surprised to discover that Aleksandr Dancek was assigned to room 209, the room next door to Ziggy and Frank.

"Hot tea for breakfast?" Joe asked as he lifted the steaming cup of brown liquid.

"I think our hosts are trying to let us experience as much of British culture as possible," Petra said and then sipped her tea.

"British culture isn't going to satisfy Joe's appetite," Frank said with a straight face.

They finished the small breakfast of tea, toast, jam, and cereal and headed out of the dining hall. Joe was still hungry and was already looking forward to lunch.

They walked out of the dining hall in silence. It was a crisp Monday morning. The fog had lifted to the top of the spires and towers, and the sun was trying to burn off the gray haze.

"I'd like to meet the wise guy who decided to schedule sculling lessons in the morning instead of during the afternoon, when it's warmer," Joe complained.

The International Classroom students were required to take one academic and one sport class. Joe and Ziggy had signed up for sculling—competitive rowing—while Frank and Petra had enrolled in fencing. The morning athletic classes began at nine and ended at eleven-thirty. Students could then eat lunch in the dining hall or in town. The afternoon academic classes, from one until three, were seminar-discussions rather than lectures.

"I'd also like to know how much physics they think they can teach us in two short weeks," Joe said, referring to the physics class he and Petra were scheduled to attend in the afternoon.

"I don't think the idea is to teach, but to discuss new ideas," Frank said.

"Yes," Petra agreed. "We young people are the future, and it is good that we are getting together now to discuss sports, politics, art, and other concerns. We do not want to repeat the mistakes of the past."

"Let's hope not," Joe said.

Frank nudged Joe and nodded his head to the left. Joe fell behind with Frank while Ziggy and Petra walked ahead, joined by other students.

"What's up?" Joe whispered.

"After sleeping on it, I think our hypothesis is all wrong," Frank replied.

"I agree," Joe said. "The idea of the Gray Man being involved in the kidnapping of a Russian teenager sounds crazy."

"Did you see Aleksandr this morning?" Frank asked.

"No."

"He's assigned to the room next to Ziggy and

31

me. He was listening to our conversation last night."

Joe turned his head to look at Frank. "Are you sure?" A slow anger was rising in Joe.

"Reasonably sure. Just keep a close watch on Ziggy."

"I'd rather watch Petra," Joe said.

"What did you say, Joe?" Petra asked, turning around.

Joe flushed with embarrassment. "I, uh, just said, 'See ya, Petra.' Here's the gymnasium."

"Goodbye, Joe." Petra said. "I'll see you and Ziggy at lunch." Petra looked at Ziggy, her eyes wide and commanding. "And stay out of trouble."

Ziggy rolled his eyes at Petra. "Yes, Mother." He nudged Joe and laughed. Then Ziggy and Joe turned down a path leading to the school's dock on the Thames River.

"I think they get along quite well," Petra said as she and Frank entered the gymnasium. Then, unexpectedly, she asked, "Does Joe have a girlfriend in Bayport?"

"No," Frank replied quickly and with a smile. While his answer wasn't exactly the truth, it wasn't a lie either. Joe didn't have a girlfriend in Bayport; he had several girlfriends.

"That's nice," Petra said, and went into the girls' dressing room.

They met several minutes later, wearing the white tennis shoes, white knee socks, white knickers, and white jackets of the sport of fencing.

Frank looked around the old but well-maintained gymnasium. The floor and bleachers were made of oak and ash and were highly polished. Windows high up in the gym provided a steady stream of morning light.

One odd thing about the gym, Frank thought, was the absence of basketball nets. The Brasenose gym was used for traditional British sports, like fencing, not for American games like basketball.

"This outfit feels like a straitjacket," Frank said with a laugh, adjusting his white fencing jacket.

"Have you not fenced before?" Petra asked.

"Yes. But it was some time ago—and in a suit that fit." Frank looked up into the bleachers, where the other students had gathered. "Looks as if you're the only girl," he said, indicating the others.

Frank and Petra joined the five other students, all boys, who were sitting together in the bleachers, talking and looking around.

Petra was adjusting the straps of her mesh mask, before putting it on. Frank thought he read worry in her eyes.

"You'll do fine," he said.

"I'm sure I will," Petra said with a sly smile.

"Good morning, gentlemen," said a tall man in fencing gear as he approached the seven students. He was taller than Frank, broad-shouldered and square-jawed, with deep-set eyes. Something about the man looked familiar to Frank. "And lady," the man added with a nod toward Petra. "I am Mr. Fitzhugh. You know me as the director of the International Classroom. I will also be your fencing instructor. It is a pleasure and an honor to welcome each and every one of you here."

Fitzhugh went on to explain that the students would study electrical fencing as opposed to dry fencing. In dry fencing, the athlete used a rubber-tipped foil and relied on the honesty of the opponent and the astute observation of the judge. In electrical fencing, the foil was plugged into a small transformer. Each fencer wore a vest—known as a lame—woven with metal wires. The foil's tip was spring-loaded. When it touched the vest, the metallic lame would close a circuit and one of two lights would flash on. A green light meant the hit was valid. A white light signaled an off-target hit.

"I know from your résumés," Fitzhugh continued, "that all of you have fenced in your own schools, and so I will not insult you by reviewing the basics. Limber up and we'll begin our first match in ten minutes."

"Hey, aren't you Frank Hardy?" one of the students asked as Frank stretched his legs.

Frank looked up. The student had dull blond hair that fell to his shoulders in thick strands.

He seemed older than the other students and had a mustache that looked more like a piece of dirty old carpet than hair.

"Yes," Frank said.

"Hey, man, I'm Chris St. Armand. From California." Chris held out his hand.

"Nice to meet you," Frank said, grabbing Chris's hand.

"Your brother's my roomie."

"I see." Frank twisted to the side, stretching his muscles.

"Yeah. You know, your brother is one uptight dude. I know what his problem is, though."

"What?" Frank said, wishing he was somewhere else talking to anybody but Chris St. Armand.

"He needs to learn to skateboard. You know, ride the concrete curl. Do three-sixty ollies. Feel the wind in his hair." While he talked, Chris pretended he was skateboarding.

"Who's your friend?" Petra asked as she joined Frank and Chris.

"Petra, this is—" Frank began.

"Wow, a fencing chick. Far out."

Fitzhugh cleared his throat and spoke. "Very good, students," Fitzhugh said. "Who wishes to be one of the first contestants?"

"I do, sir," Petra said, stepping forward.

"Me, too," Chris said, hopping into the fencing lane and jumping up and down.

Fitzhugh frowned at Chris. "Yes, well, all right."

Petra entered the fencing lane.

"Don't worry," Chris said to Petra. "I'll take it easy on you."

"Thank you," Petra said without emotion.

Petra and Chris adjusted their lames and slid their wire mesh masks over their heads and faces. Chris also put on black gloves. Gloves were optional in fencing.

"*En garde,* chick," Chris said, taking his stance, his foil in his left hand.

"*En garde,*" Petra said. She crouched.

Frank couldn't see her face, but from the cold tone of her voice and the confident and strong way she held herself in her stance, Frank could tell that Chris St. Armand was in for a fight.

Fitzhugh gave the signal. Chris lunged forward with a sweeping motion. Petra moved to her left and brought her foil over and down. The tip hit in the center of Chris's lame, where the heart was located.

"Hit!" Fitzhugh cried out as the green light flashed on Chris's side.

The first match had taken just under one second.

Chris flipped up his mask, his face red and angry. He stared at Petra, then turned, swinging his foil in a deadly arc.

"Good job," Frank said as Petra got a drink from the refreshment table.

"He is too sure of himself," Petra replied. "And not too sure of me." She smiled.

Frank looked past Petra at Chris. He was standing at the end of the fencing lane, next to the electrical transformer into which his foil was plugged.

Petra returned to her spot on the fencing lane, and they began their second match. The winner of two out of three matches would be declared the victor.

Chris began more seriously and fended off Petra's thrusts. He countered with downstrokes that were quick and displayed a fury that had been lacking in his first match. Petra had to retreat, regroup, and then attack again and again.

Chris backed up, his foil held down, giving Petra a clear shot. Petra lunged. Chris twisted to his right, and Petra's foil missed his chest. Then he flipped his foil to his right hand and pressed the tip against Petra's wire mesh mask.

Sparks flew from the mask and the foil.

Petra screamed, dropped her foil, and tried to pull the mask from her head.

The transformer hummed, then smoked, and sparks flowed out like a fireworks fountain.

Frank sprang from the bleachers and ran toward the pair. Chris let go of his foil, but it stayed attached to Petra's mask, the foil acting as an arc welder.

Frank swung his foil in a downward stroke and knocked Chris's foil to the floor.

The sparks stopped, and the transformer sputtered one last time before dying out.

Petra crumpled to the floor. Frank carefully and slowly slid the mask off as Fitzhugh and the other students gathered around.

Petra's face was ashen, and she wasn't breathing.

Chapter

5

"THE ANCIENT AND DARK Thames River runs through the center of Oxford and has helped to shape the city's history since the first Celtic warriors settled on its fertile banks fifteen hundred years ago.

"The inhabitants have always been fiercely independent people, and Oxford was a hotbed of dissent during many of England's internal wars. The people have exercised their independence in regard to the mighty Thames as well. During its short course through Oxford, the Thames is called the Isis, named for the Egyptian goddess who gave birth to the other gods."

Joe wondered why the instructor was droning on about the history of the river when all Joe wanted was to learn to be a better sculler.

The sculling instructor was a thin, pale man whose voice was more annoying than commanding. He came only to Joe's chin. His hair was dark and shiny from the hair cream that kept it flat against his head. His name was Mr. Lewis, and Joe wondered if the anemic-looking man could even lift an oar, let alone row a boat.

And it was chilly. Joe and the other students, numbering an even twelve in all, were wearing white shorts, light blue T-shirts, and deck shoes. A slight breeze off the river also clothed them with a layer of goose bumps.

Real smart, Hardy, Joe thought. You stand out here shivering your bones while Frank's inside a warm gym with the prettiest girl on campus.

"You there, young man," Mr. Lewis was saying.

Joe had been staring at the coffee-colored Thames, his eyelids growing heavy from the hypnotic effect the slow-moving and steady river had on him. The Thames was peaceful and calming. Joe shook his head and looked up. Lewis stared back, his lips white from being pressed tightly together.

"Yes, you, young man," Lewis said, pointing a bony finger at Joe.

"Yes, sir," Joe said.

"Are you interested in learning to scull or merely sleeping the day away?"

The other students snickered.

40

"Mr. Lewis," Joe said clearly, "I'm interested in learning to scull the Isis, not write a history paper on it."

Several students, including Ziggy, laughed out loud.

"That will be quite enough!" The students stopped abruptly. Mr. Lewis walked up to Joe. "So you would like to scull, Mr., uh . . ."

"Hardy," Joe said.

"An *American*," Lewis replied. Joe didn't like the accusatory tone in the man's voice.

Joe stared down at the man. "Yes, sir. And I'd like to scull very much."

"Then scull you shall."

The instructor walked past Joe to a two-man boat bumping up against the dock. The boat was ten feet long, pointed at both ends, and narrow, just large enough to hold two people. Sculling was named for the oars—sculls—used in the sport. The object was to follow a course, and the first to cross the finish line was declared the winner.

"I believe you have made him angry," Ziggy whispered as they walked to the scull.

"Don't worry. I can handle anything he dishes out," Joe said with confidence.

Lewis was sitting patiently in the boat. As Joe stepped into the boat, it rocked to the right. Joe lost his balance and fell into the chilly Isis.

He surfaced a second later, choking and spitting out water.

41

"Wow! This is freezing!" Joe shouted.

The students on the dock erupted in laughter.

"You must learn to get into the scull before you can properly handle one," Mr. Lewis said, his voice and face lacking emotion.

Joe swam to the dock and pulled himself up. He wasn't sure, but Joe suspected Lewis had purposely tipped the boat.

Joe kept his eye on Lewis as he slowly climbed into the bow. Mr. Lewis sat in the stern.

They rowed out to the middle of the river.

"We will take the short course, since you are a beginner," Mr. Lewis said.

"I've rowed before," Joe replied, frowning.

"If you insist. The advanced course it is, then," Mr. Lewis said calmly. "I will call cadence. That means I will keep time."

"I know what it means," Joe said through clenched teeth. He was freezing, and he had to force himself not to shiver, at least not in front of Lewis.

They approached the starting line at full oar—full speed. Joe counted and synchronized his breathing with every third stroke.

"Stroke . . . stroke. Stroke . . . stroke," Lewis called out in a steady rhythm.

Joe's arms began to burn. This is crazy, he thought, we must be rowing one stroke every two seconds. Joe hadn't stretched, and his muscles were resisting his commands for more power and more speed.

Lewis increased the tempo. "Stroke, stroke, stroke."

Joe pushed and pulled faster. Sweat fell from his brow and stung his eyes. He lost count of his breathing and began to gasp.

Joe couldn't believe his ears when Lewis increased the speed again.

Joe's head began to ache. Breakfast hadn't been very filling, the morning was chilly, he was soaked to the skin, and a mouse of a man was putting Joe through a mean workout.

"Faster, Mr. Hardy," Lewis said steadily, as though he wasn't even breathing hard. "Port!"

Joe eased up on his port oar and pulled harder with his starboard oar. The scull smoothly turned and glided around a small buoy. They were half-way through the course.

Lewis kept up the insane cadence. "Stroke, stroke, stroke."

Joe's muscles began to tighten. He regained control of his breathing. He strained at the oars, calling up reserve energy. His heart beat madly, and the sound echoed in his ears.

Just when he thought he could go no farther, Lewis yelled, "Oars up!"

Joe lifted his oars, straining to keep them erect.

They glided to the dock. The students were laughing and clapping and pointing at Joe.

Lewis hopped from the boat. Joe pulled himself up and stepped onto the dock, small cramps gripping the muscles in his legs.

"You did quite well, Mr. Hardy. For an American." Lewis was beaming with a broad, thin-lipped smile.

Joe was annoyed by the continuing laughter of some of the students.

"What's wrong?" he asked no one in particular.

"You were rowing by yourself," one student answered in a Spanish accent.

"What?" Joe turned to Lewis, shaking with anger.

Lewis just stood there with his thin smile and oil-slicked hair, beaming triumphantly at Joe.

Joe sighed and turned to find Ziggy. But Ziggy was not in the crowd of students.

"Have you seen Ziggy?" Joe asked the Spanish student.

"Who?"

"Pyotr," Joe said.

"He is talking to a man," the student said. He pointed behind him. "Over there."

Joe looked past the student. Ziggy was talking to Aleksandr behind a light blue Ford sedan about thirty yards away. Ziggy kept shaking his head and waving his hands in a negative manner.

Joe pushed his way through the students and walked slowly toward Ziggy and Aleksandr. He didn't like the way Aleksandr was pointing at Ziggy in short, jerky jabs, and as Joe got closer, he could hear Aleksandr speaking in an angry voice.

Joe also noticed that the blue sedan was not empty. Two men sat in the car, one behind the steering wheel, the other in the rear, his back to Joe.

The driver was facing Joe, his arm resting on the back of the seat. As Joe walked nearer, the driver got out of the car. He was an older man, tall with white hair and a hard look on his face. The driver reached into his jacket and pulled something out. Joe immediately recognized the object the driver held at his side. It was a 9-mm Beretta automatic pistol.

The man in the backseat waved at the driver, and the driver holstered his gun and got back inside the car.

Joe suddenly realized that this was the same car Frank had seen near the alley last night. Joe began to trot over to the car.

Aleksandr turned and spotted Joe. Then he grabbed Ziggy, pushing him toward the car. Ziggy resisted and tried to pull away.

"Hey!" Joe shouted, and began an all-out sprint.

Aleksandr twisted Ziggy's arm behind his back and shoved him into the backseat. He then jumped in and slammed the door shut. Ziggy was now between Aleksandr and the other man in the back. A man in a gray suit.

The car lurched forward as Joe reached it.

"Hey!" Joe shouted again and pounded on the trunk lid of the blue sedan.

Ziggy continued to struggle with Aleksandr and the other man in the back.

The car pulled away from Joe. Joe jumped and landed on the trunk. He gripped the sides of the car to keep from falling off.

"You!" Joe shouted.

The man who had remained in the backseat of the car suddenly turned around. Joe gasped as he recognized the ordinary features of the Gray Man.

The car turned sharply to the right, and Joe flew off the trunk and rolled several times across the brick road.

Chapter

6

PETRA GASPED and began coughing.

Frank raised his head. When he noticed that Petra wasn't breathing, Frank had begun mouth-to-mouth resuscitation.

Petra opened her eyes. "What happened?" she asked weakly.

"You got a little jolt," Frank said. "How do you feel?"

"I feel as if I have been kicked by a horse."

Frank helped Petra sit up slowly. She rubbed the back of her neck.

"Will you be all right?" Fitzhugh asked.

"Yes. Thank you," Petra replied, still weak.

Frank helped her to stand.

"Very good." Fitzhugh turned to the other students. "Find a partner and work on drills for the time being." He turned to Frank. "That was quick and accurate thinking, Mr.—"

"Frank Hardy," Frank said. He looked among the students and suddenly realized that Chris had conveniently disappeared.

"Ah, yes, from the United States."

"Right." Then Frank said to Petra, "You'd better sit down." He helped her over to the bleachers.

"Thank you," Petra said. "What happened?" she asked again.

"This young man saved your life," Fitzhugh replied. He held up Petra's fencing mask. The wire around the right cheek area was charred and melted. "In another second or two this would have burned through to your skin."

"I do not understand," Petra said.

"I think I do," Frank said. He walked over to the transformer Chris's foil was plugged into. He yanked the plug from the wall, picked up the transformer, and returned to Petra and Fitzhugh. "The juice on the foil was turned up all the way."

"Goodness," Fitzhugh blurted, his eyes wide circles of concern. "That's never happened before! What an accident!"

Petra gasped.

"I hope the young man wasn't harmed," Fitzhugh said. "I wonder where he's gotten off to." Fitzhugh headed for the locker room.

Frank waited until Fitzhugh had left the area.

Then he turned to Petra and said, "I don't think this was an accident."

"What?" Petra asked. Frank could tell that the bravery she had shown in fencing was replaced with the fear she had displayed the previous night.

Frank sat next to Petra, the transformer in his hands. "These things don't turn themselves up. I think Chris turned up the power all the way."

"Why?"

Frank smiled. "I think you embarrassed him with that first hit."

"I had no intention of embarrassing him. I was only doing my best."

"I know," Frank said, smiling. He stood. "I suggest we find Chris and explain to him about the need to display good sportsmanship."

"No violence," Petra said, standing.

"No," Frank replied. "Just a little persuasion."

Frank didn't want to say anything else to frighten Petra, but he didn't like the coincidence of the attempted kidnapping the night before and the attempt to hurt Petra that morning.

Chris was nowhere to be found in the gymnasium, so Frank and Petra changed back into their street clothes and left.

Petra wanted to rest, so Frank walked her back to her room and then headed for the docks. He wanted to check up on Joe and Ziggy. He hopped down the stairs and ran into Joe, who looked as if he had been run through a blender on high speed.

"What happened? Where's Ziggy?" Frank asked when he noticed that Ziggy was not with Joe.

"That's what I'm going to find out after I wash up and change," Joe said heatedly as he headed for his room. "We were right all the time: the Gray Man *is* involved in trying to kidnap Ziggy."

"How do you know?" Frank followed Joe up the stairs and down the hallway to their rooms.

"Because I saw the Gray Man, Aleksandr, and another man kidnap Ziggy!"

Joe quickly explained about the sculling lesson. Then he told Frank how he had watched helplessly as Ziggy was abducted.

"Aleksandr may be a double agent," Joe spit out. He fumbled for the room key in his pocket.

"Well, stay tuned, buddy," Frank announced. "Petra had a close call, too."

Joe turned to look at his brother, his blue eyes flashing anger.

Frank calmly explained about the fencing "accident."

"Petra's okay," Frank concluded. "She's resting in her room."

Joe unlocked the door and threw it open.

"What the—" Joe gasped.

Frank looked into the room. He'd seen beaches after a hurricane that looked better than Joe's dorm room. Joe's clothes and other belongings had been thrown around the room. All the drawers had been pulled out and tossed about.

"Someone's been searching the room," Joe said as he stepped around the debris.

"More like destroying the room," Frank replied.

"His things are gone," Joe announced.

"What?"

"Chris's things are gone. This is all my stuff."

"That kind of narrows down the suspects, doesn't it?" Frank said. "We've got to call the authorities."

"Who? The Gray Man has the Network behind him," Joe fired back. "He's got enough resources to fight off an army."

"How about the Soviet embassy," Frank suggested. Then he spotted an oblong object on the floor and picked it up. It was a cigarette lighter. He began to read the inscription.

"Excuse me." A voice came from behind Frank and Joe.

They spun around. Frank shoved the lighter into his front pocket. Aleksandr stood in the doorway.

"You!" Joe shouted, lunging at the Soviet attaché.

Aleksandr gasped as Joe jerked him into the room and kicked the door shut with his heel. He held Aleksandr by the lapels of his jacket.

Joe's voice was a low growl. "You've got

some explaining to do, and you can do it with or without your teeth.''

Aleksandr showed no emotion, no fear. He stared blankly back at Joe and said flatly, ''I prefer to speak with my teeth.''

''Wise decision.'' Joe let go of Aleksandr.

The Russian straightened his collar, tie, and jacket. The man kept his eyes on both of the Hardys and spoke in a slow, thick Russian accent.

''Let me begin by saying that Pyotr and Petra Zigonev are safe. You are not to worry.''

''Petra's gone, too? Why did you kidnap them?'' Joe demanded.

Aleksandr was unmoved by Joe's outburst. ''They are not kidnapped. They are safe. It was necessary to take Pyotr and Petra to a safe place so they could be briefed.''

''About what?'' Frank asked. He leaned against the empty dresser, his arms crossed.

''Mr. Gray said you could be trusted,'' Aleksandr said, looking relaxed now. ''I am not so sure. You are young.''

''You're the one who needs to earn our trust,'' Joe said. ''Frank and I were trying to help Ziggy and Petra. We don't know you from Peter the Great.''

''Why are you, a Soviet KGB agent, working with an American Network agent?'' Frank asked calmly.

"How did you know I was KGB?" Aleksandr asked tersely.

Frank smiled. "I didn't. Until now."

Aleksandr frowned. "Mr. Gray warned me to beware of you. He says you are cunning."

"It figures that the KGB could be working with the Network, although I don't know why," Frank replied.

"Nor shall you. Not yet," Aleksandr said. He shifted his weight. "What do you know about Sergei Zigonev, Pyotr and Petra's father?"

"That he is a KGB administrator who specializes in communications," Joe answered. He remained squared off in front of Aleksandr, his muscles tense, ready to move quickly if Aleksandr tried anything.

"Yes. Pyotr would have told you that much."

"What else should we know about him?" Frank asked.

"Sergei Zigonev is involved in delicate negotiations with American and British authorities to establish a communications link between our countries." Joe looked confused. "An open telephone line, if you will," Aleksandr explained. "So we can call each other and ask about the weather."

"For what purpose?" Frank asked.

"That is classified," Aleksandr said, his brown eyes looking past Joe to Frank. "*Glasnost* has transformed my country, and we are reaching out to the rest of the world."

"So what's the problem?" Joe blurted. "You took Ziggy and almost killed me, all because you wanted to reach out and touch the rest of the world with a telephone call?"

"This is the problem." As Aleksandr began to explain, there was a tiredness in his voice, but his sharp features had relaxed. "We have learned that not everyone is happy with the new relationship between the USSR and the West," he said. "These people would like to see the negotiations break down and the tensions between our countries rise again."

Frank pushed off from the dresser and stood next to Joe. "And the best way to do that is to kidnap a national hero. Especially a teenage national hero."

"You are correct. Pyotr is admired and adored by our leaders and by all of his countrymen," Aleksandr explained. "He is a symbol of our hope for the future, and he is an example for others. If anything were to happen to him here on British soil, in a foreign country, after he has been befriended by two Americans—"

"Then the negotiations will be called off and the old cold war started all over again," Frank concluded.

"It is probable," Aleksandr said.

"What is the name of the organization that wants to harm Pyotr?" Frank asked.

"We know of no name," Aleksandr replied.

"Only of their intent. Our information is sketchy at best."

"That still doesn't explain where Ziggy is," Joe said, resuming his hard stare.

"If you wish to see Ziggy, I am instructed to take you to him."

Joe's anger flared up. "Why didn't you say so in the first place?" Joe pushed past Aleksandr, opened the door, and started down the hallway.

Joe was waiting outside when Frank and Aleksandr left the building. The afternoon sun, at its zenith, was a bright yellow, beating back the few clouds that hung over the Brasenose dormitory.

"Why didn't you try to help us last night with the two men in the alley?" Joe asked sharply as they walked down the sidewalk that ran alongside the building and led to the parking lot. Joe stayed on the outside, with Aleksandr in the middle and Frank closest to the dormitory.

"We were about to do just that when we noticed that you had the situation under control. We left to follow the two men, but they had disappeared."

"Did you find them?" Joe asked.

"No," Aleksandr replied.

"Who was the third man with you?" Frank asked.

Gray dust floated down in front of Frank's face, and he blinked his eyes, wiping at the dust. He looked up. One of the stone gargoyles perched on top of the four-story Brasenose dormitory teetered back and forth.

"Look out!" Frank heard Joe shout.

Frank looked up to see the large gray mythical beast—with the face of a toothy, smiling demon, the wings of an eagle, and the legs of a lion—swooping down on top of him.

Chapter
7

FRANK FELT HIMSELF being pushed from behind. He sprawled onto the grass, sliding on the well-mown lawn. He heard a crash and then several thuds. Small, sharp shards of stone hit Frank in the arms and face. He jumped up and turned.

"Are you okay?" Joe asked, a haze of stone dust enveloping him.

"Yeah," Frank answered, brushing himself off. He looked behind Joe. "Aleksandr!"

The Russian lay on the ground, covered with stone dust, one large piece of the gargoyle lying by his head.

Frank pushed past Joe and ran to Aleksandr. He turned the Russian over. His face was scratched, but he appeared to be okay.

"I think I pushed him too hard," Joe said as he joined Frank. "I shoved both of you at the same time. I think he hit the sidewalk instead of the grass as you did."

"Well, he's out cold," Frank announced.

Joe looked up at the top of building. A dark head peered over the edge of the roof.

"You!" Joe shouted, and pointed. Frank followed Joe's gesture. The head disappeared. "I'm going after him!"

Joe bolted into the dormitory. He had to fight his way through the people trying to get outside to look at the accident.

Joe grabbed a short, bald man wearing wire-rimmed glasses. "How do I get to the roof?" he shouted.

"Up—up those stairs," the man stammered.

"Any other way up or down?"

The man shook his head. "No. Only those stairs."

Joe let go of the man and bolted up the stairs. "Coming through!" he shouted as he dodged several more people coming down the stairwell.

He got to the third floor and slipped going around the landing, knocking down another man.

"Sorry," Joe yelled without breaking stride as he leapt up the steps.

He reached the fourth-floor landing and turned. Something below caught his eye. The man he had just knocked down was staring up at him, a crowbar in one of his black-gloved hands, his face covered with sweat and the black and gray stubble of a two-day beard. The cap he was wearing made his head appear flat on top. He was the stocky older man from the alley.

"You!" Joe shouted, and he bounded down the stairs.

The man threw the crowbar at Joe.

Joe jumped to one side, slamming into the tiled wall. The crowbar hit the stairs and clanged down to the third-floor landing.

The man darted down the stairwell. Joe jumped the remaining stairs and then headed down to the second floor. The man was short, overweight, and looked to be in his fifties, but he was fast.

He ought to be, Joe thought. He's running for his life.

"Stop that man!" Joe ordered as they reached the crowded first-floor lobby.

But everyone moved aside, out of the way of the fleeing man, giving the thug a clear path to freedom.

"I . . . said . . . stop!" Joe yelled, and he lunged at the man, hitting him at waist level with a backbreaking tackle.

The man seemed to bend into a sideways V as his feet slid out from under him and he bent over backward. They hit the well-waxed wooden floor with a fleshy smack and slid several yards before crashing into a wall. The stocky man's head hit the wall, and he groaned and went limp. He was unconscious.

"Are you all right, sir?" a young woman asked, her face showing shock and confusion.

'Yes," Joe said, standing and brushing himself off. "Did anyone call the police?" he asked the astonished crowd.

"I did," said an older man. He opened the can of tomato juice he was holding. "Would you mind telling me what's going on here?"

"May I have that juice?" Joe asked the man, trying to sound as calm and polite as the circumstances would allow.

The man hesitated, looked at his tomato juice, then at Joe's smiling but determined face. "Well. I suppose. If you must."

"Thanks," Joe said, grabbing the can. He tilted the can and poured the cold juice onto the stocky man's face.

"I say," the older man complained, flustered. "That was perfectly good juice."

The stocky man gasped for air as the juice hit his face.

"On your feet, creep," Joe ordered. He reached down, grabbed the man's collar, and lifted him. "Where's your partner, flathead?"

The man only gurgled tomato juice. "Can't . . . breathe," the man gagged in a gravelly voice.

"Get up!"

The man stood, his legs wobbly, and faced Joe.

He rubbed his throat and gasped for air, avoiding Joe's fiery blue eyes.

"Why'd you try to kill us?" Joe demanded to know.

"I'm afraid I will have to ask the questions," a deep male voice said behind Joe.

Joe spun around. A man in his early fifties wearing a well-fitting blue English police officer's uniform stood with his hands clasped behind his back. Another police officer stood at his side. Joe acknowledged the authority etched into the man's face and voice and moved aside.

"Thank you, Mr. Hardy," the police officer said. He pointed to the stocky man. "Take that man into custody, Officer Blake.

"Yes, sir," Officer Blake responded. "Come along, you." Blake grabbed the thug by his collar and all but dragged him out through the front doors.

"How do you know my name?" Joe asked the police officer.

"Oh, sorry," the man said, watching Blake and the small man. He turned and held out his hand. "I'm Commander Collins, Oxford police."

Joe grabbed the man's hand and shook it.

Collins continued. "I spoke with your brother outside. He said you had gone after the man suspected of having vandalized the building."

"I don't think vandalism was what he intended," Joe remarked as they headed for the doors.

"Yes, well, we'll have to find out about that, won't we?" Collins smiled. In a way, the Oxford police commander reminded Joe of a friendly Chief Collig back in Bayport.

A friendly Chief Collig? Joe thought with a shudder. That's a contradiction in terms. Maybe I got hit in the head with that crowbar.

Joe found Frank standing next to Aleksandr. The older Hardy was giving a statement to another English police officer.

"You look okay," Joe said to Aleksandr.

"I understand that I have you to thank for saving my life by shoving me onto the sidewalk," Aleksandr said coldly.

"Hey, you don't have to thank me," Joe said with an edge to his voice. "It was either eat a little concrete sidewalk or get eaten by a one-ton gargoyle." Joe nodded at the shattered statue.

Aleksandr looked as if he wanted to strike out at Joe. Instead, he turned to the police officer interviewing Frank and said, "You know you cannot hold me?"

"Yes, sir," Collins replied. "You are free to go."

Aleksandr walked away from the group.

"You're not going to let him go, are you?" Joe all but shouted.

"Aleksandr has diplomatic immunity," Frank replied.

"Oh," Joe said with disgust. "We're going with him." Joe wanted to find Ziggy.

"Sergeant," Collins said to the other police officer. "Take these two young men to headquarters and hold them until I arrive."

"Yes, sir," the sergeant said with a salute. "This way, gentlemen." The sergeant pointed toward a blue and white panel van marked Oxford Police Department.

"What's wrong, Joe?" Frank asked in a low voice as they neared the panel wagon.

"I don't like the idea of Aleksandr not being questioned," Joe replied in the same low whisper. "And the guy who tried to do us in with that gargoyle is the same guy who tried to kidnap Ziggy last night."

"I recognized him when they brought him out," Frank replied. "Perhaps we can question him on the way to the police station."

Joe liked the idea. They would be alone in the back of the van with the stocky man on the ride to the station. That would give them plenty of time and opportunity to find out what was going on and whom the man worked for.

But when the sergeant opened the door, Joe saw that the back of the panel van was empty.

"Where's the other guy?" Joe asked.

"I'm afraid I don't know what you're talking about," the sergeant replied.

"The man my brother caught trying to escape

after he knocked that gargoyle off the roof,'' Frank explained.

The sergeant smiled. "I'll never understand American humor. You two young men are the ones being arrested."

Before Frank and Joe could say anything, he shoved them into back of the panel wagon.

Joe sprawled and slid across the metal floor. Then he heard the door shut. The inside of the van was pitch dark. A distinct click resounded throughout the back of the panel wagon.

"Hey!" Joe shouted. He darted for the back door and yanked on the latch. "It's locked!" He pounded on the windowless panel door. "Let us out!"

The van's engine turned over, and an overhead light came on, nearly blinding Frank and Joe. Then the van lurched forward, throwing Joe against the back door.

Joe stomped up to the front of the van. He pounded on a metal sliding panel. "Hey! What are you doing?"

The panel slid open. The sergeant was driving and Commander Collins sat in the passenger seat.

"I'd advise you to be seated," Collins ordered.

"What's going on? Why are we under arrest?" Joe demanded to know.

"Sit down, now!" Collins pointed a black steel pistol at Joe's face.

Joe backed up, his hands raised. The panel slid shut and was locked.

"What's going on?" Joe asked, looking at Frank, who was seated on the metal bench welded to the side of the panel van.

"From the looks of things," Frank replied calmly, "I'd say we've been arrested."

"Why would the Oxford police want to arrest us?

"I wouldn't know about the Oxford police. But these guys want to question us." Frank locked his hands behind his head.

"What are you talking about?" Joe sat across from Frank.

"Did you notice what kind of gun that commander pointed at you?"

"I got a real good up-close and personal look," Joe said sarcastically. "A nine-millimeter Beretta. What about it?"

"First of all, English police officers are not issued weapons, not even commanders. Second, that particular make of Beretta is a fifteen-clip special that's custom-made for one organization: BCI—British Counterintelligence."

"So these guys aren't Oxford police, and we're not going to the Oxford station," Joe stated.

"Right." Frank sniffed. "From the smell of things, I'd say we're in the country."

Joe sniffed, too. "Smells like a stockyard," he said, wrinkling his nose.

They rode in silence for a few minutes, and then Frank pulled the cigarette lighter from his pocket.

"Where'd you get that?" Joe asked.

"I found it in my room just before Aleksandr showed up." Frank turned the lighter over.

"Chris smoked. That's one thing we argued about last night." The previous night seemed a lifetime away, and Joe wished he had kept a better eye on the skateboarder from California.

Frank handed the lighter to Joe. "I think you'll find the inscription very enlightening."

Joe frowned at Frank's pun. He turned the lighter over and read the inscription: " 'Chris St. Armand, *Ne Plus Ultra*.' "

"Recognize the emblem?" Frank asked.

Joe looked at the front of the lighter. A green shield with a blue cross in the center dominated the front of the lighter. *Ne Plus Ultra* was written in the horizontal band of the cross.

"The Network emblem," Frank said. "*Ne Plus Ultra*, Latin for 'perfection.' The Network's motto."

"St. Armand is a Network agent," Joe stated with disgust. "An old-looking student."

"And a young-looking Network agent," Frank added.

"We've been set up, brother," Joe announced.

The van came to an abrupt halt. Joe heard large wooden doors being opened. Then the van moved forward slowly and stopped again. Joe heard a squeal as the doors were shut.

The light in the van went out as the engine was shut off. The Hardys sat still and kept quiet, barely breathing.

Joe could hear voices but couldn't distinguish any words. Suddenly the back door of the van flew open. A large spotlight filled the van with a blinding white light. Joe raised one hand to shield his eyes against the bright assault of the spotlight.

Moments later two large shadowy figures stepped in front of the spotlight and approached the van.

Joe was set to leap from the van and attack when he saw the silhouettes of the small Uzis the two men held at waist level. Their snub-nosed barrels were aimed at Joe and Frank.

Chapter

8

"ARE THESE THE TWO young Americans you wanted?" Commander Collins asked as he stepped between the men with the Uzis and into the spotlight.

"Yes. These are the two," replied a familiar voice.

"The Gray Man!" Frank shouted, and he and Joe hopped from the van.

"Frank, Joe," Ziggy called out as he ran up to his friends. He was still dressed in his sculling outfit.

"Ziggy!" Joe replied. "Are you okay?"

"Yes." Ziggy broke into a wide smile, as though he were greeting long-lost friends. "Petra is here, too."

Petra joined the young men. "Mr. Gray brought

me here," she explained. She looked tired but no longer as pale and scared as when Frank had last seen her.

"Speaking of Mr. Gray," Frank said. He looked past the two men with the Uzis and into the darkness behind the spotlight. "You want to explain what's going on?"

The Gray Man walked slowly up to the teenagers. "I suppose I owe you an explanation."

"That would help," Joe said, sarcasm etched in his voice.

"Perhaps I should." Fitzhugh, Frank's fencing instructor, stepped into the spotlight.

Frank could see another man standing behind the spotlight but did not recognize him.

"You're a part of this?" Frank asked Fitzhugh, watching as the unidentified man moved toward the group.

"Worse than that," Fitzhugh answered. "I'm the agent in charge."

"Agent in charge?" Frank didn't like the sound of that.

"Let me reintroduce myself," Fitzhugh said to Frank. "David Fitzhugh, vice-commander, Her Majesty's Counterintelligence, retired."

"Britain's version of the Network," the Gray Man said.

"As well as dean of continuing and special education, Oxford University," Fitzhugh added.

The unidentified man stood next to Fitzhugh. The bright light bounced off his white hair and created a halo effect around the man's head. He was as tall as Frank, and his suit was expensive.

Frank stared at the third man. "And you are . . . ?"

"Nikolai Krylov, Soviet embassy, London," the man said without hesitation in near-perfect English.

"We met earlier," Joe said with a frown. Krylov had been the third man in the blue sedan.

"KGB?" Frank said.

"Very perceptive, Mr. Hardy," Krylov said with a smile.

"You think we could shut off that light?" Joe asked, raising his hands in front of his eyes.

"Yes," Fitzhugh said. "I suggest we move this meeting into the house."

Fitzhugh nodded. The two men with the Uzis walked to the barn doors and pushed them open. One man flipped off the spotlight.

"This way, please," Fitzhugh said, motioning to the teenagers.

They walked out into a well-kept barnyard. Frank could now see that they were about half a mile from the main road. Although the place gave the appearance of a farm, Frank noticed that it lacked farm equipment and animals.

They walked silently toward a small house, whose white paint looked fresh. The lawn in front of the house was also well-maintained.

The front room into which they walked was unfurnished, and with the four teenagers and three agents, it was crowded. They all remained standing. Commander Collins and the others remained outside.

"Now that the introductions are out of the way," Joe said, "would someone mind explaining what this is all about?"

Krylov thrust his hands into his pockets. "This is about the safety and security of the world, my young American friend."

"We haven't established the fact that we're friends," Joe replied evenly.

Krylov chuckled. "No. We haven't. And perhaps we could have handled this a little better, but we"—he nodded at the Gray Man and Fitzhugh—"felt it necessary to keep you, all four of you, uninformed as long as possible."

"What makes it necessary to tell us the truth now?" Frank asked.

"The attempted kidnapping last night and the attempt on your lives this afternoon."

"*Our* lives? Aleksandr was the target." Joe was incredulous.

Krylov frowned. "Surely you do not think Aleksandr Dancek was the intended target of the gargoyle."

"What?" Petra asked. "A gargoyle?"

Joe looked into Petra's blue eyes. "One of the statues on top of the dorm building. It was loosened and pushed down by one of the men who tried to kidnap Ziggy last night."

"Aleksandr was bringing us to you," Frank explained to Ziggy.

"Why would the man try to kill Frank and Joe?" Ziggy asked Krylov.

"Your two new friends helped you last night," Krylov replied. "They are in the way."

"Whose way?" Frank asked.

"In the way of the men who are trying to kidnap Pyotr," Krylov replied flatly.

"That doesn't answer my questions." Frank returned Krylov's hard stare. "And it doesn't explain why three top secret agencies have suddenly become best friends."

The Gray Man spoke for the first time since entering the house. "We received intelligence reports in Washington that your young friend was to be the target of a kidnapping."

Frank sighed with impatience. "You're not telling us anything new."

"You must realize," Krylov began, "that Pyotr is a national hero. If anything were to happen to him, the people of the Soviet Union, despite their newfound love for Western culture and ideas, would be very upset."

"There are those elements," the Gray Man continued, "who would like nothing more than to slam the iron curtain shut once again."

"And what better way to destroy the increasingly friendly relationship between the Soviet Union and the West than by kidnapping a young Russian hero on British soil?" Fitzhugh added.

"And the attack on Petra this morning?" Joe blurted out. "Is anyone concerned with her safety?"

"What attack?" the Gray Man asked, agitated.

"It was an accident, not an attack." Fitzhugh explained about the fencing foil and the transformer box. "The student responsible for the accident has been dismissed from the school."

The Gray Man's eyes widened, and he fired back a question: "Why wasn't I informed?"

"I was told about it," Krylov answered, "and I agreed with Fitzhugh. It was an accident."

The Gray Man locked eyes with Krylov, and Frank could feel the tension between the two agency directors.

If the Gray Man didn't know about the accident, Frank thought, perhaps he doesn't know about Chris St. Armand or the Network cigarette lighter. The lighter suddenly felt conspicuous in Frank's pocket.

"Why didn't you just assign a couple of agents to escort Pyotr and Petra around Oxford?" Joe asked.

"We did. Two of our best. Aleksandr and Katrina Dancek," Krylov answered.

"What?" Ziggy all but shouted. "We have been chaperoned by KGB agents?"

"Is it so terrible for your government to want to protect you?" Krylov asked in a patronizing tone.

"No, but we do not need the secret police to watch out for us," Petra said angrily.

"I don't know what glass bubble you've been living in," the Gray Man said to Ziggy, "but the world isn't as sugar-coated as you would like to believe."

"Her Majesty's government would not have permitted the Zigonevs to participate in the International Classroom without certain assurances and assistance from the Soviet government," Fitzhugh added.

Krylov cleared his throat and smiled at the twins. "You would not have been allowed to leave the Soviet Union unless we were assured that you would be safe."

"You haven't done a very good job," Frank said.

Krylov's smile dropped to a frown. His dark eyes became slits of anger.

"I think what Frank means," the Gray Man interjected, "is that he'd feel better if we would let him and Joe in on our plans."

That's not what I meant, Frank thought, but he understood that the Gray Man was only trying to lessen the tension that had slowly been reaching the boiling point the past few minutes. Frank didn't like loose ends, he didn't like sloppy detective work, and he was not impressed with the three agencies' handling of the operation.

"Right," Frank agreed.

The Gray Man shifted his weight. "At first, we thought the Assassins were behind the reports we received in Washington."

"What made you change your mind?" Frank asked.

"The man you helped capture at Brasenose," Fitzhugh answered, "is not a member of the Assassins or any other terrorist group that we are aware of."

"A new terrorist outfit," Frank suggested.

"Maybe," the Gray Man said with a shrug.

"To be perfectly honest," Fitzhugh sighed, "we are puzzled."

"Who is the man you arrested?" Frank asked.

"A local petty hood named Howard Markham," Fitzhugh responded. "Until last night, he was more of a nuisance than a real threat."

"And what about his partner, the younger man?" Ziggy asked.

"Same thing," Fitzhugh replied. "They are both on their way to London for interrogation."

Frank decided to shift gears. He was sure that there was more to the kidnapping than they were letting on.

"What's so important about the communications linkup Mr. Zigonev is working on?" Frank asked casually.

Krylov choked and coughed. His dark eyes glanced from Gray to Fitzhugh with a nervous twitch. Then he said, "We cannot divulge classified information."

But Frank had already gotten the answer he wanted: the communications link had something to do with the attempt to kidnap Ziggy.

"What do we do now?" Petra asked, concern in her voice.

"It is best that we all act as though nothing has happened," Krylov said. The incident at Brasenose had nothing to do with the International Classroom or with Pyotr."

"I can put a security blackout on the press by using the national security act," Fitzhugh said.

"No," Krylov said, shaking his head. "The British press will know something is afoot if you do that. They will alert their American colleagues, and the American press cannot be silenced by British paranoia."

"I don't like it," the Gray Man said. "Pyotr ought to remain in a safe house, under cover, until we discover who it is that wants to kidnap him."

"No," Krylov said with conviction. "His sudden disappearance would arouse suspicion."

The Gray Man raised his eyebrows at Krylov. Frank could tell the American agent was trying to control his temper.

Gray turned to Frank. "Can you two watch over them?"

"Yes," Frank replied without hesitation.

"We couldn't do any worse than you three have done so far," Joe added.

"I still don't like it," Gray huffed.

"You will see, my friend," Krylov said, as though he were talking to an underling. "We will capture our villains."

"At what price?" Frank asked. He didn't like Krylov's patronizing attitude or the way the older Soviet agent was bossing the others.

"What do you mean?" Krylov returned, staring darkly at Frank.

"Why are you so insistent that Ziggy and Petra remain in the open?" Frank watched closely for a reaction from Krylov but saw none.

"It is best this way," the veteran spy replied evenly.

"For whom? For you? You're using two Russian teenagers as bait to lure this new terrorist group out in the open," Frank said bluntly.

"Frank!" the Gray Man cried out.

Krylov hesitated, then laughed. "You have seen too many American spy movies, my friend."

Krylov took a deep breath, smiled, and spoke in a soft voice that carried the weight and authority of an experienced spy who had survived the cold war.

"The world is not yet stable. If anything happens to Pyotr Zigonev, the Russian people will demand immediate and possibly irrevocable action. Our countries will once again be in a perpetual state of nuclear paranoia. The slightest nervous twitch from either side could send the world up in a nightmare of nuclear war."

Chapter

9

THEY RODE IN SEPARATE CARS back to Brasenose: Frank and Joe with Fitzhugh and the Gray Man, Ziggy, and Petra with Krylov.

Frank mulled over Krylov's doomsday prophecy of increased world tensions if anything happened to Ziggy. Or is Ziggy the real target? Frank asked himself. Just who is Sergei Zigonev, what is this classified communications link, and why is it so important?

Once back at Brasenose, Fitzhugh wanted to assign Aleksandr to Ziggy's room and move Frank out, but Joe was able to persuade the British agent to move Joe into the room and leave Aleksandr in his own room, next door. That way, Frank and Joe would be there if Ziggy needed protection.

A reluctant Fitzhugh had a cot moved into the room.

They had arrived back at Brasenose at five-thirty. Fitzhugh had provided a weak but adequate reason for the absence of the four teenagers from their afternoon classes: they had been special guests of Fitzhugh for an afternoon tea.

The shattered gargoyle had been cleaned up, and the college had returned to normalcy.

The four teenagers ate in the Brasenose dining hall, joined by Katrina and Aleksandr. Aleksandr's face was bruised from his spill on the sidewalk, and he avoided looking at Frank and Joe during the meal.

Joe was disappointed when Petra announced that she was going to turn in early. She and Katrina excused themselves and left the Hardys, Ziggy, and Aleksandr at the dining table.

"I think Joe likes my sister," Ziggy mused, nudging Frank to look at his brother.

Joe suddenly realized that he was staring after Petra and turned his gaze to his cup of tea.

"You do realize, Joe," Frank teased, "that you two live half a world apart, not to mention that she's got more class than you."

"Knock it off," Joe fired back, frowning.

Ziggy laughed.

"Where did you go after the accident?" Frank asked Aleksandr.

"That is none of your business," Aleksandr replied sternly.

"Got something to hide?" Joe added, lifting his eyes from his tea to stare at Aleksandr.

Aleksandr returned Joe's steely stare but said nothing.

"Why were you listening at the door last night?" Frank continued.

"I did not know you and did not trust you," Aleksandr replied. He lifted his glass and drank some water. "Now that I do know you, I still do not trust you."

"Why?" Ziggy spoke up, angry. "What have they done? Joe saved your life."

"They are Americans," Aleksandr spit out. "That is enough."

"That might have been a good enough answer five years ago," Ziggy shot back. "But it is not good enough now. Your attitude is as archaic as the Berlin Wall."

Aleksandr threw his napkin on the table. "The wall served a useful purpose." He rose and stormed away from the table, bumping into several empty chairs, nearly tipping them over.

"Touchy," Joe said with a smirk.

"He is living in the past," Ziggy said, looking down at the table. "He wants the iron curtain back. The gray matter between his ears is rusted iron, not brains."

Frank laughed. Ziggy looked up, and the tension on his face melted into a smile.

"Krylov said there was some dissent in your

country over the reforms your government is implementing," Frank stated.

"Yes, much more than you may realize. There has been talk of civil war." Ziggy picked up his tea and drank.

"Is that why the communications link between the Soviet Union and the United States is so important?" Frank asked, trying to sound nonchalant.

Ziggy smiled. "You must be a good chess player, Frank. You have an unnerving way of asking small questions to achieve big answers. However," Ziggy continued with a sigh, "I do not know what my father's negotiations involve. Excellent try, though." Ziggy rose. "I need to shower."

They walked in silence back to the second floor room. Frank stopped and knocked on Aleksandr's door, but no one answered. Frank wasn't so sure that the room was empty, though.

Ziggy took a shower while Joe made up his cot.

"This cot isn't going to be comfortable," Joe remarked. He smoothed out the wrinkles in his sheet. "You going to explain it to me or what?"

"What are you talking about?" Frank asked. He lay on his bed, his legs crossed, his hands locked behind his head.

"Why didn't you mention the lighter to the Gray Man?" Joe stared at his brother.

Frank continued to lie on the bed. He took

the lighter from his pocket. It was an old silver Zippo. He flipped the lid open, flicked the roller with his thumb, and watched as a flint spark set the alcohol-soaked wick on fire. He let it burn, then flipped the lid shut.

"I think the Gray Man is lying. Or he knows more than he's willing to tell," Frank said, returning the lighter to his pocket.

"Evidence?" Joe asked.

"Hunch. If there's one person who would know that St. Armand was a Network undercover agent, it's the Gray Man."

"Maybe Fitzhugh also knew," Joe added, testing the strength of his cot by sitting on it and then bouncing a little.

"After learning that Fitzhugh is a BCI agent, I wouldn't doubt if this place was crawling with agents," Frank said.

"And I still don't trust Aleksandr," Frank continued. "Twice today we saw Aleksandr get angry. First when the gargoyle fell, and then at the dinner table."

"I don't think he likes Americans," Joe said, satisfied that the cot would hold him.

"He had no reason to be angry," Frank said. "Unless we're not all on the same side."

Joe shot Frank a knowing look.

Ziggy emerged from the shower dressed in a T-shirt and jeans, his wet hair sticking up in spikes in all directions.

"Hey, Frank," Ziggy said, toweling dry his head. "Would you like to play chess?"

"Yeah, right," Frank said wryly.

"I'll spot you my bishops," Ziggy offered seriously.

"I don't mind sympathy," Frank said, swinging his legs over the edge of the bed and standing, "but I don't take pity from anybody. Get out the chess set." Frank smiled at his opponent.

A knock diverted their attention to the old wooden door of the room.

Joe hopped up from the cot. "I'll get it," he said in a low voice.

"Wait," Frank whispered, and he moved to one side of the door.

Joe waited until Frank was in position next to the door, then opened it.

Petra stood in the hallway, sleepy-eyed and smiling.

"Hello. I couldn't asleep," she explained.

Frank relaxed and returned to help Ziggy set up the chess set on the room's lone desk.

"Come in," Joe said without hesitation.

"Thanks." Petra walked into the room, and Joe shut the door.

"Where's Katrina?" Ziggy asked.

"She is asleep," Petra replied.

"You walked over here by yourself?" Joe's voice and eyes showed concern.

"I know I shouldn't have, but I wanted to talk to someone." Petra smiled. "Someone my age."

"I'm just what the doctor ordered," Joe replied.

"I see Ziggy has talked Frank into playing chess," Petra said with a nod toward the two players.

"Yeah," Joe replied as he pulled two chairs around to face each other. "I was wondering how I was going to entertain myself while those two spent the next two hours playing—"

"It will not take me two hours," Ziggy announced, a mischievous look on his face.

"I'm going to send your pieces to chess heaven," Frank replied with confidence.

"—but now I have someone to talk to."

Joe and Petra sat.

"It is cold," Petra said with a shudder, crossing her arms.

"I'll turn up the furnace." Joe rose and walked over to the wall furnace. Brasenose had no central heating, only old furnaces fueled by natural gas.

Almost as cozy as a real fire, Joe thought. He returned to his chair. Petra had curled up in her chair, her legs tucked under, her arms crossed, her shy smile of thanks sending warm shivers through Joe.

"Hello," Ziggy said, holding out his hand to Frank as they sat across from each other. "My name is Sitting Bull, and you are General Custer, I presume. Welcome to Little Big Horn."

Frank only smiled. As white, he moved first.

He placed his king pawn in king four position. A typical opening move. Ziggy countered with the same but opposite move with his black pawn.

"Give up," Ziggy joked.

"Die, Russian dog," Frank fired back, moving his queen knight directly in front of Ziggy's pawn.

"I don't know if I can take all this excitement," Joe said. "Ziggy seems more like a showman than a champion chess player."

"I believe you call such behavior 'hamming it up,' " Petra said with a laugh. "This could take hours."

Joe smiled and thought, I hope so.

An hour passed quickly. Frank and Ziggy were malicious in their playing, intensely scheming before making each move, teasing each other, threatening each other. At times, Joe wondered if a chess match or a shouting contest was in progress.

Joe and Petra spent the time talking about American boys and Russian girls, rock and roll, and the trouble with parents.

Joe yawned in the middle of a sentence. "Excuse me," he said, embarrassed.

Petra covered her mouth as she yawned, too. "Must be contagious." She nodded toward Frank and Ziggy.

Joe noticed for the first time that the chess players were silent and wondered when the shouting had stopped. Their heads were lowered, and Frank and Ziggy looked as though they were asleep.

Joe turned back to Petra. She had fallen asleep. I'm losing my touch, Joe thought, a thin haze covering his eyes. He blinked and tried to shake himself awake. His head began to ache with a slight but persistent pounding around the temples.

Then he noticed the room was still cold.

Joe slowly turned his head toward the furnace. The fan was softly blowing. He stood, his legs going out from under him. As he fell, he hit a small tea table, then landed on the floor.

Sleep. He wanted to sleep.

He crawled and pulled his way to the furnace. He yanked on the small vent door at the bottom of the furnace. His fingers were numb, and he lost his grip on the metal knob. After several tries, the door sprang open.

Joe looked inside. The furnace was dark. No pilot light; no flame.

Joe's head felt heavy. He laid his head on the floor. He couldn't keep his eyes open. One thought kept trying to push its way through his brain before he lost consciousness. He had to shut off the gas before they all suffocated to death.

Chapter

10

"JOE."

The voice was far away, an echo ricocheting inside his head like an errant bullet. Joe lifted and turned his head.

"Joe."

The voice was closer.

He opened his eyes. Petra was lying next to him, her eyes watery, her breathing shallow.

Joe pushed up, every fiber of his muscles screaming for oxygen. He crawled over to the window, grabbed the windowsill, and pulled himself up. His arms were leaden, tight, and stiff. Once he was on his feet, he tried to push the window up, but it was locked. He looked out through the panes.

Students strolling in the chilly evening were

distorted by the glass and the foggy haze that drifted through Joe's mind.

Joe pounded on the window, but he was too weak to make any real noise. He looked down. Ziggy's wet towel was on the floor. He grabbed the towel and wrapped it around his hands. He held his breath, balled his hands together, brought them back over his head, and swung them forward in a swift, powerful arc.

His towel-covered fists hit the window, shattering the glass. Clear shards fell to the sidewalk below and broke again. Several students turned at the bell-like sound of glass crashing on the concrete.

Joe hit the window again. More glass went flying out and down, hitting the concrete with a dull tinkling.

Fresh air poured into Joe's lungs, and he gasped for more.

"Help," he said, his voice barely audible. Joe leaned toward the broken window, his legs like warm taffy, his lungs on fire, his head swimming in a dark nightmare of fog and distortion. He took a deep breath and screamed, "Help!"

Then he blacked out.

The first thing Joe saw when he came to was a dull white light in the center of the room. A dark halo surrounded the light.

Joe coughed; his lungs ached. He focused his eyes. The dark halo divided into three separate shapes, and a moment later Joe recognized the distinctive faces of Krylov, Gray, and Fitzhugh.

"Leave it to a Hardy to come back from the dead," the Gray Man said with a chuckle. "Welcome back, Joe."

"Where am I?" Joe asked. His head began to clear more quickly, and the fire in his lungs subsided.

"Oxford infirmary, lad," Fitzhugh replied.

Joe looked around. He was in a double room, but the other bed was empty. A lone window had its bland yellow curtain drawn. The room was bright white and sterile-looking, and it smelled like alcohol.

"The others?" Joe smacked his lips. His throat was dry.

"They are fine," Krylov answered. "Thanks to you."

Joe pushed himself up on his elbows. "No, I mean, where are they?"

Frank walked into the room, a cold can of ginger ale in either hand.

"Hey, brother," Frank said with a grin. "I thought you'd like this when you came to."

Joe took the drink. It felt heavy, but he lifted the can to his lips and drank long and deep.

"That's good," he said after a moment, wiping his lips with the back of his arm. "Someone want to explain what happened?"

"From what the others have said," Fitzhugh replied, "it appears that you turned up the gas furnace without checking to make sure the pilot light was on. The room filled with gas and nearly killed all four of you."

"Was it just another accident that the pilot light was out?" Frank asked skeptically. "Two near misses in one day, and you're not suspicious?"

Fitzhugh coughed. "Well, I must say that it does seem rather coincidental."

"More like intentional, don't you think?" Joe said. Then he polished off the ginger ale.

"Impossible," Krylov said.

"Why?" Joe said, scooting off the bed and standing.

"We have been watching the area," Krylov responded.

"In fact," the Gray Man added, "I've been watching your room since early afternoon. No one went in or out." He chuckled. "You know you can trust me."

Frank wasn't so sure. He put his hand in his pocket and fingered the lighter again. "Where has Aleksandr been?"

"He has been called back to the Soviet embassy in London," Krylov replied.

"Why?" Frank wanted to know.

"Confidential," the Soviet agent said flatly.

"I'm getting just a little tired of this," Frank blurted.

The three agency heads stared at Frank, all looking startled.

"What do you mean, Frank?" Gray asked.

Frank looked at Krylov. "You told us earlier today that you wanted Ziggy and Petra out in the open so as not to arouse the suspicion of school officials or the press."

"What about it?" Krylov asked.

"You're just using them as bait," Frank said pointedly. "Trying to bring the kidnappers out in the open."

"Such impertinence," Fitzhugh huffed.

"And you," Frank continued, looking at Fitzhugh. "I know the English are famous as masters of understatement, but you've raised it to an art form. You explain everything as an accident or a coincidence. Just what kind of intelligence agent are you?"

"Frank!" the Gray Man barked.

"You're not innocent in all of this," Frank shot back. "I don't know what your angle is, but you've got something up your sleeve, and I intend to find out what it is. Let's go, Joe." Frank walked swiftly out of the room.

Joe followed, catching up with his brother as he headed down the stairs.

"Hey, there's hope for you yet," Joe said with a smile.

"What are you talking about?" Frank's face was flushed, and his voice was hoarse.

"I'm the one who's supposed to get angry and shoot off my big mouth, but your little outburst back there was great."

They opened the door at the bottom of the stairs and walked outside into the night air.

"Don't believe everything you see or hear," Frank said, his smile broad and devilish.

Joe showed surprise. "That was all an act?"

"Yep."

"Why?"

"I want to see who panics first." Frank thrust his hands into his pockets as they walked on.

"Far out," Joe said with a laugh. "I'd take my hat off to you if I wore a hat." Joe looked around. They had passed the Brasenose dorm and were headed east on the High. "Hey! Where are we going?"

"We've been moved," Frank explained. "We've been assigned to two guest cottages on the Corn. You, Ziggy, and I in one, Petra and Katrina in the other. Fitzhugh thought it best to keep us all together and away from the university."

Joe sighed. "Nothing like putting all your eggs in one basket and then shooting at them."

"Yeah. You still have the cot," Frank added. "Here we are."

A light blue British Ford sedan was parked across the street from the twin cottages. Two men—agents, Joe suspected—sat in the front seat. Both kept their eyes on the Hardys.

Joe was surprised at the size of the cottages. They were small, whitewashed structures no larger than a two-car garage. Each had one door framed by two small windows.

Frank pushed open the door of the men's cottage. It had two rooms. One was a large room with a sofa, an overstuffed chair, twin beds, and two chests of drawers. The cot stood at the end of the beds. The other room was a small utility kitchen with a back door. Just like some American hotel rooms, Joe thought.

"Joe!" Ziggy shouted as the Hardys entered the cottage.

"Hey, Ziggy. How's it going?" Joe looked around for Petra.

"She went to her cottage," Ziggy said with a knowing smile.

"I think we'd all better get some rest," Frank said with a yawn. "It's almost midnight, and we've got to be up in a few hours for our tour."

"Tour?" Joe asked, unbuttoning his shirt.

"The trip to Salisbury Plain," Ziggy replied, excited. "And Stonehenge."

"I'd forgotten." Joe yawned. Although he'd been unconscious for two hours, he was exhausted. "At least we won't have to worry about Lewis browbeating us about sculling."

Ziggy laughed.

"What's so funny?" Joe asked.

"Lewis is the tour guide," Frank said. "He not only teaches sculling, he is also a professor of medieval English literature and folklore. You should have read the brochure."

"Great," Joe moaned as he sank onto his cot.

Joe didn't remember going to sleep, and he didn't remember waking up. He remembered lying down and talking to Frank and Ziggy, and the next moment he realized that the room was dark and he was wide awake. He turned his head and saw Frank standing in front of one of the small front windows. The curtain was pulled open slightly, and a thin beam of moonlight highlighted his brother's features.

"What is it?" Joe asked in a whisper, trying not to awaken Ziggy.

"I think someone just panicked," Frank replied in the same low whisper.

Joe swung his legs over the edge of the cot, rose, and walked to the window. Frank stepped back to let Joe look out through the crack.

"I heard a car pull up," Frank explained. "Then two car doors slammed."

Joe looked through the crack. Joe could make out the tall form of Fitzhugh talking to two men. Joe recognized them immediately. One was Howard Markham. The other was Chris St. Armand.

Chapter

11

"DO YOU KNOW that Salisbury Plain is the legendary battleground of King Arthur and his knights of the Round Table?" Ziggy asked Joe as they approached the tour buses.

"Really," Joe said with a sigh.

All through breakfast, Joe, Frank, and Petra had listened to Ziggy as he gave them a verbal guided tour of Salisbury Plain and Stonehenge. Ziggy loved British history, Petra explained, especially medieval history, and considered the Tuesday tour to Salisbury Plain the highlight of his two-week stay.

The students climbed aboard three buses. Frank, Joe, Ziggy, and Petra sat in the back on the bench seat that ran the width of the bus. Frank sat next to Joe, who sat next to Ziggy.

Petra sat on the other side of her brother. Joe started to plan a way to get Ziggy to move so he could sit next to Petra.

Fitzhugh and Lewis sat in the front of the bus.

"I think what we've stumbled on," Frank said in a low voice so only Joe could hear him, "is the makings of a conspiracy. We're not looking for some clandestine terrorist group."

"We have found the terrorists, and they are among us," Joe quipped.

"Right."

"Do we keep this to ourselves?" Joe nodded toward Ziggy and Petra.

"We don't know who else is involved." Frank wiped the dust from his sunglasses with his shirttail and then held them up to the morning sunlight to check for cleanliness.

"You think the Gray Man is a part of this?" Joe asked.

"Why not?" Frank slid his sunglasses on and leaned back in his seat. "If the East and West become best friends, high-powered spies will be obsolete."

"You don't expect me to believe that all of this is happening so some spies can keep their jobs," Joe stated.

"I know it sounds crazy." Frank yawned.

"Crazy? Try ludicrous."

"Just the same, we can't trust anybody, not even the Gray Man. Agreed?"

"Agreed."

Frank sighed, and Joe could tell by the heavy breathing that his older brother was almost asleep.

Joe tapped Ziggy on the shoulder. "Trade seats with me, Ziggy," Joe said. "Frank wants to talk over last night's game with you."

"Sure," Ziggy said, and hopped up.

Joe was in Ziggy's seat before Ziggy realized that Frank was asleep.

"Gotcha," Joe said, pointing his finger at Ziggy like a pistol.

"I'll get even," Ziggy warned, smiling and sitting next to Frank.

By the time the buses arrived at Stonehenge three hours later, Frank had gotten a good nap, Ziggy had gotten more excited, and Joe had gotten Petra's home address.

Ziggy had understated the beauty of Salisbury Plain, which was a span of low, rolling, grassy hills. Ziggy had pointed out to Petra and Joe the many chalk carvings of horses and other animals in the sides of the hills left by Celtic and Anglo-Saxon warriors.

Ziggy was so excited about Stonehenge that he tried to be the first one off the bus.

Frank rubbed his sleepy eyes and waited to be the last off the bus. He stepped down and removed his sunglasses to get a clearer look at the ancient megaliths known as Stonehenge.

The massive stones were gray and worn down by wind and rain and time. Several stones lay on the ground and looked like large altars. Others seemed to be stuck into the ground haphazardly, at various angles, without any rhyme or reason. Some formed giant gateways, with one huge stone placed across two upright ones. The entire place was a marvel of engineering.

Lewis was speaking to the group as Frank walked up behind the students. Joe and Petra were at the rear of the crowd, but Ziggy was nowhere to be seen.

"Where's Ziggy?" Frank whispered to Joe.

Joe pointed. "Up front."

Frank stood on tiptoe and saw Ziggy at the front of the crowd, listening intently to every word Lewis was saying.

"Stonehenge stands ten miles north of the city of Salisbury and has existed for almost four thousand years. During the last century," Lewis droned on, "Stonehenge has received the greatest amount of damage from war, pollution, and people who have defaced the stones.

"The only modern structure is the iron railing used to keep people away from the stones. Although most tourists are forbidden to get too near the stones, I have received security permission to allow you students to roam freely once I have finished my lecture. Now . . ." Lewis continued, speaking on the four-thousand-year history of the stones from the beginning to the present day.

"Brother," Joe moaned after a few minutes. "I could get this stuff from a textbook."

"Yes," Petra agreed. "Mr. Lewis has a way of making this beautiful site quite boring." She turned to Joe, a sly smile on her face. "Shall we begin our tour early?"

"Just what I was thinking." Joe returned Petra's smile.

Joe and Petra slowly backed out and away from the other students.

"Where are you going?" Frank whispered to Joe.

"To get a better look at the stones," Joe answered, and he and Petra disappeared behind one of the megaliths.

Frank didn't know what Joe was up to, but he didn't like his younger brother taking such chances, especially since he suspected that Fitzhugh was a rogue agent.

Frank made his way among the other students, noting the bored, restless looks on their faces, and stood next to Ziggy.

"Isn't this fascinating, Frank?" Ziggy whispered when he noticed Frank next to him.

"Uh-huh." Frank sighed. Listening to Lewis was like playing a scratchy old record that skipped.

"It's almost as if these stones are giant chess pieces," Ziggy whispered.

Frank smiled. "Played by ancient Druid mystics and Celtic priests."

"This gives me an idea." Ziggy took a small notebook from his pocket, sat down on the grass, and began scribbling. "Would you like to play chess tonight?" Ziggy didn't look up.

Frank knelt beside Ziggy. "Are you kidding? You were leading me to slaughter before our little accident last night."

"Yes, but I think you will find tonight's game fascinating." Ziggy scribbled on.

"What are you working on?" Frank leaned over to look at Ziggy's notebook.

"Excuse me, gentlemen," Lewis said loudly. "But would you mind paying a little more attention to the lecture."

"I'm taking notes," Ziggy lied, smiling at Frank.

Frank stood up. "Sorry," he mumbled.

They spent another fifteen minutes listening to Lewis before the group was dismissed to explore the stones.

Frank was eager to find Petra and Joe, but he didn't want to leave Ziggy, who still sat on the grass scribbling in his notebook. Also, Frank wanted to examine the stones himself. He would hate to have come all the way to England without getting a good look at one of the world's truly great mysteries.

An hour later they were all on the buses, headed to the city of Salisbury to eat lunch before returning to Oxford.

Frank explained to the others that Salisbury was famous for its many spires and the orderly way the city had been laid out in a grid. Although Salisbury had been designed hundreds of years before, the city still followed the same basic plan.

"Nice and orderly and logical," Frank concluded.

"There's that steel-trap mind again," Joe said with a laugh.

Frank frowned at his younger brother.

The students were allowed to eat at any one of the many pubs and sidewalk cafés, as long as they were back at the buses by one-thirty.

Frank, Joe, Ziggy, and Petra decided on a small café away from the main street. They scanned the menu.

"I wonder where Fitzhugh is going," Frank said.

Joe looked up. Fitzhugh was on the other side of the street, walking quickly. He disappeared inside a shop with its name hand-printed in white letters on the picture window: Stonehenge Antiques.

"I think I'll check out some of the local artifacts," Frank said to Joe. "Order for me."

Frank glanced both ways and then crossed the street. He didn't know what, but something about Fitzhugh bothered Frank.

Frank walked up to the old shop and pushed open the door, causing a bell to clang.

"May I help you?" asked a short, bald man from behind the counter. He had been leaning on the counter, reading a newspaper. His skin was wrinkled and mottled, and he looked to be in his seventies.

Frank glanced around the small shop, which was cluttered with rusted tools, old baby carriages, and stained tables. An assortment of stuffed animals hung on the wall.

"I'm with the students from Oxford," Frank explained. "I'm looking for Mr. Fitzhugh, our program director. He just came in here."

"I'm sorry," the old man said. "You are the only customer I've had in the past hour."

"I'm sure I saw him come in here," Frank insisted. "A tall, broad man with dark eyes."

The old man slowly shook his head. "No. As I was saying, you are the only living soul I've seen in an hour."

"Thank you," Frank said with a sigh, and left, the bell clanging again.

Frank spotted Joe across the street at the café. Joe nodded his head. Frank shrugged his shoulders, then pointed to an alley.

Frank walked into the alley, which ended at a brick wall. He knew Fitzhugh had gone into the shop and then disappeared into the back of the store, but why was the old man hiding that fact? Frank wanted to find a side door and perhaps sneak in.

He walked to the middle of the alley. There was an olive drab door on rusty hinges. Must be the one, Frank thought. He put his hand on the knob and turned. The door was locked.

"Look who we have here, Chris," came a voice from behind Frank.

Frank spun around. Howard Markham and Chris St. Armand stood at the head of the alley.

"We have ourselves an alley cat," St. Armand sneered.

"Hi, guys," Frank said calmly. Then to St. Armand he said, "Tear up any rooms lately, Chris? Or do I call you Agent St. Armand?"

"What?" St. Armand asked, puzzled.

Frank pulled the Zippo lighter from his pocket and held it up.

"Where'd you get that?" St. Armand spit the question out.

"On the floor where you left it," Frank replied.

"Give it back to him," Markham ordered.

"No," St. Armand said. "I want to take it away from him—after I tear him apart piece by piece."

St. Armand started down the alley, a dark scowl on his face.

Frank moved to the center of the alley and took a defensive karate stance. St. Armand was the same height and build as Frank. And although he was Network trained in fighting, Frank knew a few tricks, too.

St. Armand stopped five yards from Frank. He laughed. Then he reached over his back and inside his jacket collar. He drew out a short but shiny and deadly Japanese sword.

"Piece by piece," St. Armand hissed.

Chapter

12

FRANK BACKED UP to the brick wall at the end of the alley. St. Armand approached slowly but with confidence.

"I understand you're good at fencing, Hardy," St. Armand said. "How are you with real swords?"

St. Armand swung the sword in a horizontal arc, the razor-sharp silver blade hissing through the air.

Frank jumped back and hit the wall. The blade came so close to Frank's face that he could feel a slight breeze from its edge. St. Armand followed through with his strike, swung the blade over his head and then down. Frank shifted to one side and crouched down. The blade hit the wall, sending sparks and small sharp shards of brick flying in all directions.

Frank lashed out with a kick to St. Armand's right kneecap. St. Armand's right knee bent to the side and then back, forcing St. Armand to back up.

St. Armand grunted.

Frank knew he hadn't broken the knee, but he could tell by the grimace on St. Armand's face that the blow had caused a good deal of pain.

Frank grabbed a crate and threw it. St. Armand slashed at the wooden crate, shattering it with his sword.

"You're next, Hardy," St. Armand fumed as he approached Frank.

"Hey! Chris!" Joe yelled from the head of the alley.

St. Armand spun. Markham lay on the ground, unconscious, Joe standing over him. Joe stepped over the older man and walked toward St. Armand.

St. Armand turned back to Frank, but Frank had already made his move. A solid right to St. Armand's left cheek knocked him to the ground. St. Armand tried to raise his sword, but Frank stepped on St. Armand's wrist.

Frank put his full weight on the wrist until St. Armand opened his hand and let the sword fall out. Frank grabbed the sword and pointed it at St. Armand.

"Stand up," Frank ordered.

"You okay?" Joe asked as he joined Frank.

"Yeah."

St. Armand stood, favoring his right leg.

"What brings you to this neck of the woods?" Frank asked.

"I'm looking for antiques," Joe said. "I saw you go into that shop, then come out and walk down this alley. Then these two came out of the shop and followed you. You set a nice trap."

"I didn't trap them. I didn't even know they were in the shop. The only one I saw was an old man sitting behind the counter."

"Lucky for you," Joe began, "that I'm a detective."

Frank smiled and shook his head.

"Now what?" Joe asked, looking at St. Armand and then at Markham, who was still unconscious.

"If I were back in Bayport, I'd take these two to the police station. But I don't know that I trust the local English police after yesterday."

"No kidding," Joe said.

"Let's see what secrets this antique shop has." Frank pointed the sword at St. Armand's stomach. "Unless you want to become a shish kebab, I suggest you behave yourself."

"And when we're done with whoever's inside," Joe added, glaring at St. Armand, "I've got some questions about a little fencing match."

Joe walked over to Markham, shook him awake, and pulled the groggy thug to his feet.

They all walked into the antique shop as though they were tourists.

"Remember me?" Frank asked the man behind the counter, who was still reading the newspaper.

"Yes," the man replied dully. He looked at St. Armand and Markham but showed no reaction. "Did you find your friend?"

"No, but I found these two," Frank replied. "What's in the back?" He jerked his head toward the rear of the store.

"My home," the old man said.

"Mind if we look around?" Frank didn't wait for an answer. He shoved St. Armand toward the beaded curtain that covered the doorway at the rear of the shop.

While Frank guarded St. Armand and Markham with the sword, Joe looked around. The back of the shop consisted of several rooms containing some old furniture, a few pictures on the wall, and little else. No Fitzhugh. No clandestine meeting room. Nothing but an old man's home.

"Is there something I can help you with?" the old man asked from behind the group.

Frank turned. The old man stood in the door, an old 9-mm Beretta in his hand and a hard look in his eye. Frank recognized the Beretta as the special fifteen-clip model made for BCI agents.

"Drop the sword," the man ordered in a soft but commanding voice.

Frank tossed the sword, and it slid under the sofa.

"I owe you this," St. Armand said as he drew back his fist to punch Frank.

"That's enough, St. Armand," the old man barked. "You two young Americans have been interfering in our plans, and it is time for you to stop." The man spoke with dignity and authority, and St. Armand obeyed him without question.

"Why do you want to hurt the Zigonevs?" Frank asked.

"That is of no concern to you," the old man said calmly.

"We're making it our concern," Joe blurted out.

"Then you, too, will have to die," the old man said evenly.

He pulled a silencer from his pocket and screwed it onto the barrel of the black Beretta. He raised the gun shoulder high and aimed it at Frank's forehead. The old man showed no emotion, but the cold hard stare of his gray eyes sent a shudder through Frank.

Frank had seen the look before, the cold, calculating, unemotional look of a professional killer.

Chapter

13

THE BELL on the shop door clanged.

"Is anybody here?" Ziggy asked at the top of his voice.

Joe heard several students talking and walking around the shop. The old man hid the Beretta beneath his sweater.

"I think I've seen enough," Joe said loudly as he headed for the beaded curtains. He stopped and stared down at the old man. "You have nothing that interests me." Joe pushed through the curtain. Frank followed.

"This isn't over yet, Hardy," St. Armand said through gritted teeth.

Frank turned and peered back through the strings of beads. "When it is," Frank warned, "you'll be the first to know, and I'll be the one delivering the message to you."

St. Armand moved to Frank.

"Easy," the old man said, and St. Armand stopped.

Frank smiled and turned to join Joe.

"Hi, Joe, Frank," Ziggy said as the Hardys walked to the center of the shop. "Find anything interesting?"

"Just a bunch of junk and some rats in the back," Joe replied with a nod to the back room.

Frank watched as the old man moved through the curtains and returned to the counter. He picked up the newspaper and began reading it without looking at the Hardys, as though nothing had happened.

Frank, Joe, and Ziggy walked outside.

"I brought the cavalry," Ziggy whispered under his breath. "I didn't like the way you kept going in and out, with more desperadoes joining you each time."

"Thanks," Joe said with a smile. "Where's Petra?"

"Looking for postcards with the other girls."

Joe's eyes followed Ziggy's pointing hand. Even in a crowd of pretty girls, Petra was a gem among the other precious stones.

"Have you seen Fitzhugh?" Frank asked.

"He is on the bus," Ziggy said.

"He must have slipped out of the shop when

we were in the alley," Frank explained, shaking his head.

They boarded the bus and once again took the long seat at the back. Frank and Ziggy sat on the outside while Joe and Petra sat between them. Moments later, all three buses pulled out of Salisbury and began the long journey back to Oxford.

The other students were loud, and Frank welcomed the noise. He wanted to talk to Ziggy and Petra, and he didn't want to wait until they had returned to Brasenose. The talking of the other students provided a noisy cover.

But before Frank could say anything, Ziggy asked bluntly, "Would you mind letting Petra and me in on your little secret?"

"What are you talking about?" Frank asked, puzzled.

"As a chess player, I watch not only the board but my opponent as well. I try to read his face, see if he is nervous, overconfident, or worried. I have been watching you two, and you have not been completely honest with Petra and me."

Frank looked at Joe, who only shrugged.

"That works both ways," Frank said.

"What do you mean?" Petra asked.

The bus took a wide turn, and they braced themselves to keep from sliding across the seat.

"I don't believe that the attempts to kidnap Ziggy are only because somebody wants to ruin the good relationship between the Soviet Union and the West," Frank said.

"What do you believe?" Petra asked defensively.

"I think your father and the communications-link negotiations are part of this," Frank replied. He tried to read Petra's cool blue eyes but got only a cold stare. He looked at Ziggy.

Frank continued. "Your father is KGB and an expert in communications. He is negotiating with his Western counterparts for something. But what?" Frank hesitated, hoping Ziggy or Petra would answer. But the twins just sat pensively on the edge of their seats.

"The United States has just launched a new satellite that is designed to move communications into the twenty-first century," Frank explained.

"A spy satellite," Petra huffed. "What do friendly nations need with a spy satellite?"

"It's not a spy satellite," Frank continued. "It's a communications satellite powered by a CRAY computer, the most powerful computer in the world. While most satellites can handle thousands of bits of information a second, the new CRAY satellite can handle a billion bits of information a second."

"You are correct," Ziggy said with a sigh.

"Ziggy!" Petra cautioned.

"Frank has made the killing move and has checkmated us," Ziggy told his sister. He smiled at Frank. "Our country has always lagged behind in technology, and our people have suffered because of it. If we were allowed to come on-line with the new CRAY satellite, the Soviet Union will be able to advance in technology."

"How do we know the Soviet Union won't use the CRAY satellite to spy on the free world and its people?" Joe asked.

"My father is trying to assure your government that such a thing will never happen," Ziggy said.

"And if your father can be distracted," Frank explained, "he may fail in his negotiations."

"Correct," Ziggy said. "Father knew how important the International Classroom was to us and would allow us to attend only after he received certain assurances regarding our safety."

Petra shifted in her seat. She avoided looking at Joe. "We would not have been allowed to attend the International Classroom if Mr. Gray had not assured the Soviet officials and our father that you two would be with us."

"What?" Joe was stunned, and he stared at Petra, searching for answers.

"I think what Petra has just told us," Frank said, "is that our selection to attend the International Classroom and our room and class assignments were manipulated so that we would be with the Zigonevs at all times."

"That's incredible," Joe blurted. "Why didn't you tell us, Petra?"

"I am sorry, Joe," Petra said softly.

"Why do I feel like a pawn?" Frank asked, staring at the floor of the bus.

They rode in silence for the remainder of the trip.

Katrina met them as they got off the bus, and they all walked back to the cottages together. It was almost six, and the sun was setting.

Katrina asked Petra about the trip to Salisbury Plain, but Petra answered in monosyllables. She entered her cottage without saying anything to Ziggy, Frank, or Joe.

"Don't worry, Joe," Ziggy said as they entered their cottage. "Petra is not angry with you. She is upset because she had to deceive you."

"How do you know that?" Joe asked, sitting on the edge of his cot.

"We are twins," Ziggy answered. "Sometimes we know each other's feelings."

"Yeah, right," Joe mumbled.

"She likes you, Joe."

Joe smiled. "Thanks, Ziggy."

Frank sat in the overstuffed chair. The day's long trip and the revelation that he and Joe were being used by three covert agencies rested on him like a heavy weight.

"Hey, Frank!" Ziggy said. "Want to see what I was working on at Stonehenge?"

"What?" Frank asked, tired and wanting to take a nap.

"Your remark about the stones being giant chess pieces gave me an idea. I will call it my Stonehenge Strategy," Ziggy announced with flair.

"What?" Frank said with a laugh.

"It involves sacrificing the queen and winning the match with pawns." Ziggy began setting up the chessboard.

"Impossible," Frank said, rising from the chair. "The queen is the most powerful piece."

"That's the gambit. Want to try it?" Ziggy waved his hand at the chessboard.

"Yeah," Frank said, curiosity overtaking him.

Joe sighed. "While you two play your little game, I'm going to take a nap." He stretched out on his cot and was softly snoring a few minutes later.

Frank and Ziggy squared off again, baiting each other.

"This is like the spider and the flea," Ziggy said, a devilish tone to his voice.

"That's the spider and the fly," Frank corrected. "But 'flea' will do." Frank moved his pawn. "After I get done swatting you, I'll want you to write down your theory in English so I can take it home and put it in my computer and work out the flaws in your Stonehenge Strategy."

Ziggy tapped the side of his head. "This is the only computer worth programming."

Frank laughed, but his laugh was cut short by

a deafening blast. The cottage shook and plaster dust fell like light snow from the old ceiling.

Joe was tossed from his cot and landed face-down on the floor.

"What was that?" Joe shouted.

Frank raced to the door of the cottage, followed by Joe and Ziggy. They ran out into the dark night and headed for the twin cottage, in which Petra and Katrina were staying.

The front door was locked. Frank kicked it in.

Moonlight streamed into the cottage from a large hole in the wall against which the twin beds rested. One bed looked as if it had been cleared of the bricks that had fallen on it. A bloody leg stuck out from under the rubble of bricks that lay on the second bed.

"Petra," Ziggy whispered.

Joe and Ziggy started pulling bricks off the body and tossing them the length of the cottage. Frank pulled out his penlight and flipped it on. The circle of light illuminated the gray dust that hung in the air like a fog.

But when Joe and Ziggy had cleared away the pile of rubble, they discovered not Petra but Katrina, her face cut and bleeding, her breathing shallow.

She opened her eyes and swallowed. She turned and glanced at the other bed. Her eyes widened in fear and terror.

"Petra," she gasped. "They . . . have . . . taken . . . her!"

Chapter

14

"JOE! The wall's going to fall!" Frank shouted.

Joe gently lifted Katrina and moved away just as the wall teetered and collapsed, sending up another thick cloud of plaster dust. The bricks crushed the beds.

"Let's get her outside," Frank said, shining his light toward the door.

"Where is Petra?" Ziggy asked, his voice cracking. He refused to leave the cottage.

Frank grabbed Ziggy and pulled him out the door.

Joe had laid Katrina on the ground.

"I must find Petra!" Ziggy shouted.

"She's gone!" Frank shouted back.

"No," Ziggy whispered, shaking his head.

"How is Katrina?" Frank asked Joe.

"She's breathing," Joe replied.

Sirens split the air, and moments later the cottages were surrounded by ambulances, fire trucks, and police cars.

"You gents seem to bring trouble with you," Commander Collins said as he walked up to the Hardys. "You're keeping us rather busy."

Joe looked up. "Too busy to do your job right," Joe angrily spit out.

"What are you implying?" Fitzhugh asked as he joined the group. Krylov and the Gray Man were behind him.

Joe stood. His voice was low and had all the sting of a yellowjacket. "It's a little late for the cavalry to arrive."

"Settle down, Joe," the Gray Man ordered.

Krylov broke away from the group and walked over to the hole in the wall.

"Joe's right," Frank said, keeping an eye on the KGB operative. "You'd think the combined security agencies of three of the world's top covert groups could protect two teenagers. Where was your security force tonight, Mr. Gray?"

"It was in place," the Gray Man said flatly.

"The wrong place," Joe countered.

"I suggest we place these two young Americans under special protection," Fitzhugh said, his voice agitated and rough.

"No, thanks," Joe said. "I've seen your security measures, and I'm not impressed."

"What about Petra?" Ziggy asked softly.

"We will find her," Krylov said, rejoining the group. He rubbed his fingers together. "Whoever it was used plastic explosives."

"Is anyone really surprised?" Frank asked sarcastically.

"I will take Pyotr to the Russian embassy in London," Krylov announced. "He is not safe here."

"I wish to look for my sister," Ziggy insisted.

"You will not be able to find her," Krylov said. "And I will not take a chance on you being kidnapped, too. Come, you must pack."

Krylov grabbed Ziggy by the arm and led him to the men's cottage.

An uneasy feeling settled in the pit of Frank's stomach. Krylov was Aleksandr's boss, and Aleksandr did not like Americans or the new détente.

The paramedics placed Katrina on a gurney and wheeled her to the waiting ambulance. A respirator covered her face, and an IV bottle was feeding her glucose.

The dark night was cut sharply by the blue flashing of the various emergency vehicles' lights. Frank, Joe, and the others watched as the doors of the ambulance were shut. The ambulance sped away, its eerie wail echoing throughout the night. Commander Collins followed in his car.

"I hope Katrina is okay," the Gray Man said.

"That's just great coming from you," Joe blurted.

"What do you mean?" The Gray Man's usual dull expression was replaced by one of surprise.

"She said you took Petra." Joe stared hard and deep at the Gray Man. They had been good friends once, but now Joe felt as though he was staring at a dangerous enemy.

"That's ridiculous," the Gray Man said.

Fitzhugh cleared his throat. "Our young friends are obviously confused."

"Yes," the Gray Man agreed, nodding his head. His eyes darted from Frank to Joe. "I think it best that Frank and Joe be placed in protective custody."

"What are you trying to hide?" Frank asked the Gray Man heatedly. "Why didn't you tell us about Chris St. Armand?"

The Gray Man looked surprised. "Who?"

"He was my roommate," Joe replied.

"Impossible," the Gray Man said. "St. Armand was dismissed from service months ago."

"Why?" Frank asked.

"He tampered with some documents we had received from a field agent in Turkey," the Gray Man explained. "He and other agents were feeding the Network and BCI disinformation."

"What's disinformation?" Joe asked.

"Intentionally false information about other countries." Frank explained.

"What was the disinformation?" Joe asked.

"We should not be discussing this," Fitzhugh said. His voice sounded nervous.

"St. Armand provided disinformation that the Soviet Union was planning to crush the reform movements in Eastern Europe," the Gray Man continued. "He was hoping that the United States, Britain, and the other NATO allies would react by increasing their military presence in Western Europe, thus destabilizing the new relationship between the Soviet Union and the West."

"As well as the CRAY satellite negotiations," Frank added.

"That's right," the Gray Man said, nodding.

"You mentioned that other agents were involved," Frank said. "Who were they?"

"They were British," the Gray Man replied. He looked at Fitzhugh. "But we never caught them."

"They got out of the country before they were found out," Fitzhugh said quickly.

"How do we know that *you* didn't take Petra?" Frank challenged.

The Gray Man looked Frank in the eye. "I didn't, Frank. I'm one of the good guys."

"Why did they take Petra and not Ziggy?" Joe asked.

"They made a mistake," Fitzhugh said angrily. He turned to the Gray Man. "I still say these young men should be put in protective custody."

"I think you're right," the Gray Man said, his voice tired.

"We want to find Petra," Joe insisted.

"There are three things I don't like about you two," Fitzhugh said angrily. "You're brash, you're impertinent, you're noisy, and you're Americans."

"That's four," Frank said.

"And I'm American," the Gray Man said. "Do you dislike me as well?"

Fitzhugh's cheeks puffed out. "Hmph!" He motioned to two men standing by the blue British Ford sedan.

"Bert," Fitzhugh addressed the shorter agent, "these two young men are in need of our protective services," Fitzhugh said. "Take them to the farmhouse."

"Yes, sir," Bert replied.

"We're not going anywhere," Frank said sternly.

With surprising speed, the shorter agent grabbed Frank's arm and twisted it behind his back.

"Now, don't give us any trouble, lad," he said in a harsh cockney accent.

The second agent reached into his jacket and started to pull out a Colt .45.

"Not here, Jenkins," the Gray Man ordered.

"Yes, sir," Jenkins said. From his accent Frank guessed that he was an American.

"No need for weapons," Fitzhugh agreed. "I think our young guests realize the foolishness of resisting."

"Okay," Frank said, and Bert released him.

"I want to help find Petra!" Joe wasn't ready to give in so easily.

"I'm sorry, Joe," the Gray Man said. "The stakes are too high."

Bert and Jenkins pushed the brothers toward the sedan as Fitzhugh and the Gray Man got into another car and pulled away.

"Why are you letting Fitzhugh run things?" Frank shouted back to the Gray Man. "Why are you trying to keep us quiet?"

"Shut up," Jenkins ordered, and pushed Joe forward.

Frank felt betrayed by the Gray Man. For all he knew, Mr. Gray could be part of the conspiracy. And Fitzhugh's anti-American sentiments had finally shown through. In fact, Fitzhugh sounded like a British version of Aleksandr.

The British agent who worked with St. Armand was never caught! The thought struck Frank like a thunderbolt. And why was Fitzhugh so sure that the kidnappers had made a mistake in taking Petra instead of Pyotr?

"It's your fault," Frank angrily said to Joe.

"What?" Joe's voice registered shock and confusion.

"It's your fault," Frank repeated. "If you'd done your job, none of this would have happened."

"What are you talking about?"

Frank stopped and shoved Joe. "I'm talking

about the incompetent way you've handled this case all along!" Frank shouted. Then he winked.

Joe had to stop himself from smiling. He shoved Frank back.

"Yeah? Well, you're the moron who came up with the great idea." Joe swung at Frank.

Frank ducked and struck Joe in the mid-section.

The two agents laughed. Bert, the short one, said, "We're going to see a brawl, Jenkins. I'll wager on the blond one."

"You're on," Jenkins replied.

Frank and Joe continued to push and shove, holding on to each other's shirts, working their way closer to the two agents.

"Looks more like a wrestling match than box-ing," Bert said, disappointed. "Come on, you two, knock each other's brains out!"

"Now!" Frank shouted.

Frank landed a solid right to Bert's jaw while Joe hit Jenkins in the chest with a spinning karate kick. The agents fell to the ground simul-taneously.

"Their car," Frank said with a nod to the blue sedan.

Joe sprinted past Frank and hopped into the driver's seat—and only then remembered that the driver's seat in British cars was on the right. He scooted over, reached under the dash, and yanked down on the wires. He took out his pocket-knife and cut a large red wire, then a green wire, then stripped both of them, hoping that the wiring in British cars was the same as in American cars. After all, the car was a Ford.

Frank jumped into the passenger seat as Joe touched the wires together. Sparks flew in the darkness. The engine turned over but didn't start.

"Come on, come on," Joe ordered the engine as it continued to grind. He stomped on the gas pedal.

"Let's go, Joe," Frank said, his voice strained and nervous.

Joe glanced into the rearview mirror. The two agents were running up fast behind the car, guns drawn, Bert with a 9-mm Beretta and Jenkins with a .45 automatic.

Joe touched the wires again, and the sedan fired to life.

"Halt!" Bert yelled as he approached the car.

"We're out of here!" Joe shouted. He shifted the car into first and floored the accelerator. The rear tires spit up mud and grass as they tried to grip the ground for traction. The debris hit the two agents.

"Stop! Now!" Jenkins yelled, wiping mud and grass from his face. He leveled his .45 and fired. The rear windshield shattered.

Frank slumped down in the front seat.

Chapter

15

"FRANK!" Joe shouted above the roar of the engine.

"I'm okay," Frank said. "I'm ducking. Something you ought to consider doing."

"No need," Joe replied. "We're long gone." He shifted gears. "What's the plan?"

"What plan?" Frank asked. He sat up and looked behind him. They were driving east on the High, out of Oxford.

"You don't have a plan?" They passed Magdalen College and crossed the bridge. "You always have a plan."

Frank remained silent. They passed the neat little row of houses Frank had noticed three days earlier and were quickly in the country heading toward London.

Frank didn't like the similarities between Fitzhugh and Aleksandr. And how was St. Armand able to bluff his way onto the International Classroom rolls? Fitzhugh was the director. He had a hand in selecting students. As a BCI director, Fitzhugh had to have known that St. Armand had been fired from the Network. And the British agent hadn't been caught. Fitzhugh said Petra's kidnapping was a mistake. How did he know that?

"Where to?" Joe asked.

"I don't know yet," Frank said. "Would it surprise you to learn that Fitzhugh is behind Petra's kidnapping?"

Joe drove in silence, the wind blowing back his blond hair. A moment later he said, "No."

"You want a plan?" Frank asked, not expecting an answer. "Let's cool it for a while in the country. Then we can double back and get Ziggy out of the cottage."

"What about Petra?" Joe asked.

Frank sighed. "Whoever has Petra may use her as a bargaining chip to get Ziggy. He's the one they really want. Besides, Fitzhugh was upset and said that *they* had made a mistake. How would he know *they* had made a mistake?"

The Hardys drove around for an hour, then made their way back into Oxford from the south.

They parked the car a block from the cottage and worked their way slowly and cautiously back to the cottage, hiding in the shadows and against the buildings. They had to watch out not only for Network, BCI, and KGB agents but also for the local police. It was midnight, and Frank and Joe were behaving like criminals.

They stopped a short distance from the rear of the men's cottage.

"Can you see anything?" Joe asked.

"No," Frank replied, exhaustion etched into his voice. He squinted as he tried to see through a window of the cottage. "It's dark inside."

"You think Ziggy's still in there?" Joe was just as tired and just as anxious as Frank.

"Only one way to find out."

Frank and Joe began walking toward the cottage, the darkness providing cover for them.

"They could have moved Ziggy while we were driving around in the country," Joe said.

"That's possible," Frank agreed. "Let's keep low."

Frank and Joe bent over and scrambled the rest of the way to the cottage. They leaned against a wall, catching their breath.

"What do you think?" Joe whispered.

"Let's try the back door," Frank said.

They crouched and moved closer to the back door. Joe took out his pocketknife and slid it between the door and the jamb. A moment later he had opened the door.

They crept into the kitchen. Frank pointed toward the living room. They tiptoed to the doorway. Joe pointed to himself and then toward the living room—he was going first.

A light flared on as Joe started out into the living room.

"No need to sneak around, Mr. Hardy," Bert, the British agent, said. "Come in, please."

Bert hadn't seen Frank, so Frank began backing away from the doorway. He stopped as he felt the cold steel of a gun barrel against his neck and heard the sharp click of a hammer being locked into place.

"Not running out on the party, are you, friend?" Jenkins asked in a distinctive American accent.

Frank raised his hands and walked into the living room. Joe was standing by the couch, his hands clasped behind his head. Frank joined him as Jenkins stood beside his British partner.

"You Yanks ain't as smart as you think you are," Bert sneered, "comin' back here and all." He glanced at Jenkins. "Looks like we caught ourselves a couple of kidnappers."

"Right, Bert," Jenkins replied. "We're going to be heroes."

The men raised their guns and pointed them at the Hardys.

"Night-night, gents," Bert said, smiling, showing his teeth.

"Are you ready to die for the Gray Man?" Frank asked Jenkins.

"I'm ready to die for my country," Jenkins replied. "Just as you're about to do."

"What if the Gray Man isn't working for his country? What if the Gray Man is working for the Soviets?" Frank looked deep into Jenkins's eyes, searching for a reaction, but the agent was a veteran and his poker face was blank, hard as stone.

"You're an amateur," Jenkins said to Frank, his voice flat.

"That may be true," Frank replied. "But I'm not a traitor."

"What do you blokes mean?" Bert asked.

"We mean that someone has been manipulating events from the first day, trying to cause an international incident," Joe said.

"That's crazy," Bert blurted.

"Exactly," Frank said. "That's why Joe and I have been trying to stop it."

"Who's behind it?" Jenkins asked.

"We're not sure," Joe said. "Ever hear of a Network agent named Chris St. Armand?"

"Yeah," Jenkins said.

"He's here in England," Frank said.

"Impossible," Jenkins shot back.

"Why?" Joe could see a rising doubt in Jenkins's face.

"He was canned from the agency," Jenkins explained.

"What about Fitzhugh?" Joe asked Bert.

"What about him?" Bert kept his pistol at waist level, pointed at Joe.

"How much do you trust him?" Joe lowered his arms slowly.

"Fitzhugh's retired, only used on special occasions. He's a fine chief." Bert's voice lacked the confidence to back up his words.

"We're concerned only with the safety of Ziggy and Petra," Frank said. He, too, lowered his arms.

"We returned to find out if Ziggy was safe," Joe added.

"He's safe," Bert replied.

"He's gone with a Soviet operative to a safe house. He'll stay there until this is over," Jenkins said.

"Who's the agent?" Frank asked. "Krylov?"

"No," Bert said. "The young one."

"Aleksandr!" Joe exclaimed.

"That's the one," Bert said.

"Where's this safe house?" Frank asked.

"I think we ought to call Mr. Gray and find out what to do with these two," Jenkins suggested, glancing at Bert.

"Yeah," Bert agreed. "I don't like the look of things." He made a move toward the phone.

"You call Mr. Gray, and you'll be putting the lives of two young Soviet nationals in danger," Frank warned.

Bert's hand was inches from the phone, hovering above it, his bulldog face showing uncertainty and indecision. He unclutched and clutched his gun. Then he moved away from the phone.

"How do we know what you say is true?" Bert asked.

"This might help." Frank slowly slid his hand into his pocket and pulled out the lighter. He tossed it to Jenkins.

Jenkins caught it, turned it over, and read the inscription. "It's St. Armand's all right," Jenkins said to Bert. He put the lighter in his jacket pocket.

"Where's the safe house?" Joe asked.

Bert looked at Jenkins, who nodded.

"Fitzhugh wanted the Zigonev kid away from Oxford. He persuaded Krylov to have Aleksandr take the boy to a safe house near Stonehenge," Jenkins explained.

"Fitzhugh and Aleksandr, again," Frank hissed.

"That's too close to the antique shop," Joe added.

"Don't you see?" Frank asked the two agents. "Fitzhugh, St. Armand, Markham, and Aleksandr are all involved in a plot to destroy the relationship between the Soviet Union and the West."

"Why would they want to do that?" Jenkins asked.

"To save their jobs," Joe answered.

"I don't know if I trust these two," Bert said to Jenkins.

"What choice do you have?" Frank asked.

"How could we know about the antique shop and St. Armand unless we also knew about the conspiracy to kidnap the Zigonevs?"

"He's got a point," Jenkins said.

"A dull point," Bert countered.

Jenkins tucked his gun into his shoulder holster. "They may be teenagers," he said to Bert, "but they have a good rep within the Network. I'm willing to take a chance."

Bert reluctantly agreed. He uncocked his gun and put it into its holster.

"We'll take our car," Bert said. "I bet you two left it somewhere nearby."

The trip to the safe house took nearly three hours. Wednesday dawn was creeping over the English countryside.

Frank had wanted to see as much of England as possible during their two-week stay, but he hadn't wanted to see it in the dead of night while trying to rescue two Russian teenagers.

Bert had driven the entire way with Joe sitting at his side and Frank and Jenkins in the back. The four had had little to say to one another during the trip.

Bert parked the car half a mile from the safe house, which, Frank noticed, was another farmhouse without farm implements or animals. The house was set back from the road and was all but hidden from the highway by a windbreak of oak trees.

They circled around and came up behind the house. The early morning fog hid them as they crouched down and scampered up to the back of the farmhouse.

Frank could see that the house was made of stone, was small, and had only one story. A brown door sat in the middle of the back of the house with two windows flanking it.

They reached the back of the house without being seen and pressed themselves against the cold, wet stones.

Frank took short choppy breaths, every nerve in his body pulsing. He peeked in one of the windows. It was a bedroom, and it was unoccupied. He shook his head at Joe, who was near the other window. Joe peeked in and sent the same message back to Frank.

Bert signaled with his hand that they were going to go in through the back door. The two agents pulled their weapons out, flipped off the safeties, and cocked back the hammers.

Frank knelt and crawled to the back door. He took out his pocketknife and slid the blade between the door and the jamb. He pressed the blade against the bolt and pushed. It wouldn't budge. He applied more pressure, grimacing as he did so.

The knife blade suddenly snapped, but not before the bolt slipped out of its slot. The door popped open.

The breaking of the knife and the squeak of the door echoed in the back room.

Frank looked at Joe and the two agents. After a moment, he entered the back room, followed by the others.

It was a laundry room and pantry. Frank tiptoed to another door, opened it a crack, and peeked in. He stared into a sitting room: three armchairs, a coffee table, a fireplace, and an overstuffed couch.

On the couch, gagged and with their arms and legs tied, sat Ziggy and Petra. They appeared to be asleep.

Frank signaled to Joe, and the brothers crept into the room. Bert and Jenkins stepped in behind them, their guns pointed at a door on the far side of the room.

Frank first shook Ziggy awake. He awoke with a start and kicked out at Frank. Frank blocked the kick and give Ziggy a stern look.

Ziggy's eyes showed confusion, then recognition. Even though he wore a gag, Frank could tell that the young Russian was smiling. Frank untied Ziggy.

Joe woke Petra, who seemed to be in a state of shock.

"Joe!" Petra hoarsely whispered as Joe took off her gag.

Joe quickly pressed his finger to his lips in a signal for her to remain silent.

The door across the room suddenly burst open.

Frank turned. Fitzhugh stood framed in the doorway, an Uzi resting easily in his hands.

"Fitzhugh!" Bert exclaimed. "What the devil—"

Fitzhugh answered with an angry staccato burst of gunfire from the deadly machine gun.

Chapter

16

FRANK SHOVED ZIGGY down, while Joe grabbed Petra. All four of them landed behind the sofa, pieces of fabric and stuffing exploding around them as red-hot bullets from the Uzi tore through the furniture.

Jenkins and Bert fell to the floor and remained still.

Jenkins's Colt .45 was a yard away from Frank's reach, out in the open. Frank quickly snaked his hand out from behind the sofa, grabbed the pistol, and pulled it back in a split second.

Another burst from the Uzi shook the room and splintered parts of the wooden floor.

Frank pointed the .45 over the back of the sofa and fired in the general direction of Fitzhugh.

The Hardys heard a door slam, and then all was silent.

"Where is he?" Joe whispered.

Frank slowly raised himself up and peeked over the back of the sofa.

"He's gone," Frank replied, catching his breath.

"Joe?" Petra asked, her voice shaking with fear, her eyes full of panic.

"It's going to be okay," Joe replied with a smile, wishing he felt as confident as he sounded.

They all stood.

"*Oh!*" Petra cried out when she saw the bodies of Jenkins and Bert sprawled beside the door.

"Don't look," Joe said. He put an arm around her and led her into the laundry room. Frank and Ziggy followed.

"What now?" Ziggy asked.

Although Ziggy tried to sound brave, Joe read fear in his eyes, too. Ziggy was used to mapping out strategies and destroying opponents, but that was in chess, where no one really got hurt, let alone killed.

"We've got to get away from here, get help," Joe said.

"I wish I knew where Aleksandr was," Frank said.

"Aleksandr?" Petra's voice cracked.

"He is one of the kidnappers," Ziggy explained angrily.

"This gun's empty," Frank said, tossing the .45 aside. He crept over to the door, opened it a crack, and peered out. No one was in sight in the front room.

"What are we going to do, Joe?" Petra asked, holding back tears.

"We're heading for higher ground," Frank answered, pointing to a small hill half a mile from the "safe" house.

"Stonehenge," Joe said as he followed Frank's pointing finger to the giant ancient stones.

The morning sun hung behind the ancient stones, which appeared as black silhouettes against the mist. "There's a guard there. He'll be able to call for help," Joe said.

"My thoughts exactly," Frank agreed. "I wish that fog had stayed put a little longer."

Joe faced Petra. She was ashen, holding back tears, her lower lip trembling. She had every right to be frightened, Joe thought.

"Think you can run to Stonehenge?" Joe asked her softly.

"Y-yes," Petra replied.

"How about you?" Joe asked Ziggy.

"Yes," the young chess champion said.

"Looks as if you'll get to put your Stonehenge Strategy to a real test," Frank said with a slight smile at Ziggy.

"Let's ride," Ziggy replied. "We're burning daylight."

Frank nodded and pushed the back door all

the way open. He looked outside. Fitzhugh was nowhere to be seen. Frank stepped out, held up a hand signaling the others to remain where they were, and looked up and down the length of the house.

"All clear," Frank said. His heart was pounding, and he felt as though it would burst through his chest. He could feel the veins in his temples pulse. His breathing was short and choppy.

They crouched as they scrambled away from the rear of the farmhouse. There was nothing to hide behind between the safe house and Stonehenge. The plain gently sloped toward the massive stones.

A car engine roared.

Frank turned.

A light blue British Ford sedan, its rear windshield a spiderweb of tiny cracks, was bearing down on them.

"Run!" Frank yelled, and they all dashed in a straight line for Stonehenge.

Frank turned. The car had stopped. Fitzhugh had gotten out of the car, followed by Aleksandr, St. Armand, and Markham. They all had Uzis trained on the group.

A burst of gunfire tore through the air toward them.

"Hit the ground!" Frank yelled.

Frank dived to the ground and slid through the ankle-high, dew-soaked grass for several feet. The ground popped and exploded as bullets from the Uzi hit the earth around him. Then the firing stopped.

Frank lifted his head and turned around. The gunmen were jumping back into the car, Aleksandr driving, St. Armand next to him, and Fitzhugh and Markham in the backseat. The car lurched forward. It looked to Frank as if they were heading back toward the highway. The only consolation was that Fitzhugh and company would have to circle back and around to get to Stonehenge by way of the road. It was a good two-mile drive, but still, they would have an easy time catching up to the foursome.

"Let's go!" Frank yelled.

He jumped to his feet. Ahead of him he saw Joe and Petra leap up and continue their sprint for Stonehenge. Ziggy stood, started to run, stumbled, and fell head first to the ground.

Frank reached him in seconds. He bent down to pull the young Russian to his feet. "Let's go, cowboy!" he said.

It was then that Frank noticed the blood on Ziggy's shoulder.

"Cannot . . . go on," Ziggy moaned. His face was pale, and Frank could tell Ziggy was going into shock.

"Yes, you can," Frank ordered, his voice hard. "I'm going to beat you at chess, and you're not going to get out of it this easily." Frank helped Ziggy to stand.

"Oh, yeah?" Ziggy replied with a smile, trying to steady himself. "The only way you can beat me is if you have an extra queen up your sleeve."

"We'll settle this later," Frank said.

He and Ziggy ran for the stones. Ziggy was moving at half speed, keeping his right arm at his side. Frank could tell that one of the bullets had nicked Ziggy's right shoulder, doing just enough damage to make the arm painful and impossible to use.

Joe glanced behind him. He wondered why Frank and Ziggy were so far back. The wet grass and mud must have slowed them down, Joe thought.

Joe turned his attention to Stonehenge. They were three hundred yards from the ancient monument. He wondered where the guard would be stationed. He glanced at Petra out of the corner of his eye. She was keeping pace with him.

"Almost there," Joe panted.

"We can make it," Petra replied, her voice sounding strong.

Joe glanced back again. Frank and Ziggy were moving too slowly. The sedan had reached the highway and was speeding to Stonehenge. The teenagers would have to cross the highway to get to the ancient monument, and once on the open road, they would be easy targets for the gunmen.

A minute later, Petra and Joe had reached the highway. The sedan was half a mile away.

"Run across the road," Joe ordered Petra, pushing her out onto the deserted highway. "Find the guard. Tell him to call for help."

"I don't want to leave you!" Petra shouted back.

"I'm going to wait for Frank and Ziggy." Joe glanced down the road. The sedan was closing fast. "Go on!"

Petra stood still in the middle of the highway, unsure what to do. She turned her head toward the approaching sedan, then looked back at Joe.

"Hurry," he said. Petra raised her hand to wave, changed her mind, turned toward the stones, and ran as hard and as fast as she could.

Joe watched her until she was across the highway and among the stones. He looked to his left. The blue sedan was seconds away. He turned his attention to the ground and looked around him. He reached down and picked up a baseball-size, nearly round piece of granite. He wondered if it had once been a part of Stonehenge or was merely some leftover scrap from when the monument was built.

His attention was directed back to the sedan as it bore down on him. Markham was leaning out of the rear window, the wind pressing back his face and giving him an ugly, menacing smile. His hair flew straight back, and his Uzi was pointed at Joe.

The stone was heavier than a regular baseball,

and Joe was an outfielder, not a pitcher, but he put all his weight and best aim into the throw.

The granite baseball hit the already weakened rear windshield and knocked a giant hole in it.

Aleksandr lost control, and the sedan swerved just as Markham opened up with the Uzi. Joe hit the ground, the bullets clipping at his heels. He rolled in the wet grass and sprang to his feet as the Uzi went silent.

Aleksandr was trying to regain control of the sedan. He twisted the wheel back and forth in an effort to straighten out the car. Joe watched as it hit an embankment, rode up high on the grass, and then flipped over. The sedan landed upside down, then slid and spun with a metal scream. Finally it stopped fifty yards down the road. Engine coolant hissed as it leaked out and struck the hot engine, some turning to steam and some hitting the asphalt road.

The occupants in the car remained still. Joe didn't know if they were dead or alive, and at the moment, he didn't care. He was just glad they weren't shooting at him.

"What happened?" Frank asked as he and Ziggy joined Joe.

"I just made the pitch of a lifetime," Joe said.

"Where's Petra?" Ziggy asked, his voice weak.

"She ran to Stonehenge to get help," Joe said. Then he saw the blood. "You've been hit!"

Ziggy straightened up in an effort to appear

okay. "Just a scratch, pilgrim," he said, imitating John Wayne.

"Let's find Petra and the Stonehenge guard," Frank advised.

The three crossed the road at a trot, Joe keeping his eye on the sedan. Still, no one moved.

They hopped the iron fence that kept viewers away from the monument and headed for the inner circle of stones.

"Petra," Joe called out.

There was an uneasy silence, and then seconds later came, "Here, Joe."

"This way," Joe told the others, and he set off in a jog toward Petra's reply.

Petra was in the inner circle, at the easternmost part. The sun had risen just above the stones and was behind Petra, shining down on her blond hair.

"Petra," Joe uttered with relief and a smile.

"Joe," Petra said flatly, "I can't find the guard."

Frank and Ziggy joined them.

"Ziggy!"" Petra cried out when she saw the blood on Ziggy's shirt. She ran to her twin brother.

"It is okay, only a scratch," Ziggy said with a weak smile.

"We've got to find that guard," Frank said. "I can't believe he didn't hear that accident."

"He did," growled a voice from behind the foursome.

They spun around. Fitzhugh and Aleksandr stood twenty yards from them. Fitzhugh's 9-mm Beretta and Aleksandr's Uzi covered the teenagers.

"And now it's time to arrange another little accident," Fitzhugh said through clenched teeth.

Chapter

17

FITZHUGH AND ALEKSANDR were scratched and bloodied, their suits soiled and ripped. They glared at the group, waving their weapons between the teenagers.

An old man wearing a dark blue security guard's uniform joined them, a Beretta in his left hand.

"The old man from the antique store!" Joe exclaimed.

"Right," Fitzhugh said. "He just happened to be on duty."

"I heard the accident and came in from the opposite direction," the old man explained.

"What about Markham and St. Armand?" Frank asked.

"Dead," the old man said calmly.

"Don't you think Her Majesty will be upset when she learns that one of her trusted BCI agents was involved in a plot to kill two young Soviet nationals?" Frank asked Fitzhugh.

"Correction, Mr. Hardy of Bayport, USA," Fitzhugh said nonchalantly. "I, my Russian colleague, and Mr. Hampton here"—he nodded toward the old man—"will be rewarded for killing the two Americans who murdered Pyotr and Petra Zigonev."

"You plan on blaming their murder on us?" Joe blurted.

"Correct," Aleksandr said.

"And how do you propose to do that?" Joe asked.

"We do not have time to explain anything to you, nor do we wish to do so," Fitzhugh said. He took a white handkerchief from his back pocket and wiped his smudged and bloody face with it.

"I do not understand why this is happening," Ziggy said, his voice weak.

"It is necessary if we are to achieve our goal," Aleksandr answered.

"What goal?" Petra asked.

"You are too young to understand," Aleksandr said. "The reforms implemented in our country are evil. It is not right for our country to abandon the old ways."

"Is that what you believe?" Frank asked Fitzhugh.

"I believe in what pays the most," Fitzhugh replied calmly. "Aleksandr and those he represents have paid me well for my participation in this little escapade, and I don't intend to disappoint them."

"What about Katrina?" Petra asked, tears welling in her eyes.

"She thinks the reforms are good, that the Soviet Union ought to be more like the West," Aleksandr fired back. "She should have died in the blast."

"No!" Petra cried out.

"You will not get away with this," Ziggy stated.

Aleksandr jabbed Ziggy's wounded shoulder with the barrel of the Uzi. Ziggy yelled and fell to the ground in pain.

"You creep!" Joe shouted at Aleksandr. He knelt down beside Ziggy.

"We're walking out of here," Frank announced.

"You're what?" Fitzhugh was stunned.

"You've got two choices," Frank said. "You can kill us in cold blood here and now, or you can shoot us in the back as we walk away. How would you explain that to Her Majesty?"

"You're bluffing," Fitzhugh scoffed.

"Think so? Look into my eyes and tell me what you see." Frank squared off against the taller man. He was hoping to take advantage of Fitzhugh's confusion and weak condition.

Fitzhugh matched hard stares with Frank. "I see a dead American."

"Then you need glasses." With lightning speed, Frank planted a bone-crushing fist in Fitzhugh's sternum. Fitzhugh staggered backward, his Beretta firing into the dirt. Frank twisted and landed a spinning karate kick on the British agent's head. Fitzhugh hit the ground like a felled tree. Frank wrested the Beretta from him and threw it as far as he could.

Joe lunged at Aleksandr and grabbed him in a bear hug, pinning the Uzi in a vertical position between them above shoulder height. The Uzi exploded with gunfire as Aleksandr squeezed the trigger. The bullets whizzed into the air. The spent shells expelled from the chamber bounced off Joe's and Aleksandr's chests.

Joe continued his bear hug, squeezing Aleksandr and at the same time forcing him backward. He slammed the Soviet agent into one of the large upright stones. Aleksandr groaned above the thunderous roar of the Uzi. Joe slammed him into the stone again. He felt Aleksandr weaken. He was about to slam Aleksandr into the stone a third time when the Uzi suddenly went silent, empty of bullets.

Joe stepped back. Aleksandr stood limp, his arms at his side. He dropped the Uzi to the ground.

Joe turned around to check on Petra.

Petra had the old man in a choke hold, one

arm pinned behind his back. His gun was lying on the ground.

"You are full of surprises," Joe said to Petra with a smile. He picked up the old man's Beretta and told Petra, "I'll take care of him now."

Petra returned Joe's smile, let go of the old man, and then knelt to help her brother.

"They've been at it for two hours," Petra complained as she frowned at her brother and Frank hovering over a chessboard in the waiting lounge at Heathrow Airport.

"It's a good thing we got here early," Joe replied, "or you'd miss your flight."

"I regret missing the rest of the International Classroom." Petra sighed. "But Father feels it's necessary that we return."

"And without you here, it just won't be the same." Joe looked deep into Petra's light blue eyes.

"You are so charming, Joe Hardy," Petra said with a laugh. "I'll bet you say that to all the girls you meet."

"Only the pretty ones from the Soviet Union," Joe countered.

Petra laughed.

Joe and Petra were distracted by a yell from Frank.

"What kind of move is that?" Frank shouted as Ziggy moved his queen diagonally across from one of Frank's pawns.

"It's called strategy. Haven't you Americans learned the proper way to play chess?" Ziggy fired back.

"You're going to lose your queen," Frank announced.

"Go ahead, take her," Ziggy replied with a shrug. "I can beat you one-handed." Ziggy raised his right arm and displayed the sling that was supposed to keep it immobile while his shoulder healed.

Frank began to move his pawn, changed his mind, and set it back down. He knew that Ziggy was trying out his Stonehenge Strategy, and Frank was doing everything he could to ruin Ziggy's game.

"You must take the queen!" Ziggy shouted.

Frank smiled and moved his king bishop instead.

"You scoundrel!"

Joe rolled his eyes. Then he turned back to Petra. "What will happen to Aleksandr?"

"I hope they toss him in jail and throw away the key," Ziggy said from the table. "Check."

"Check?" Frank's eyes were wide with confusion. He studied the board intently.

"Why would anybody want to ruin the peace that has taken so long to achieve?" Petra asked.

"Because the world is full of crazies," the Gray Man answered as he joined the group, carrying a tray with a steaming pot of tea and five cups. "Then you have mercenaries like Markham, St. Armand, and Fitzhugh, who sell their loyalty to the highest bidder."

Petra began pouring the tea.

"One thing you kids have done for us," the Gray Man said, "is help us clean house. There's going to be a clean sweep from top to bottom in the Network, the KGB, and BCI."

"Some people just can't stand to see things change," Joe said to Petra. "They think that the only way to maintain peace is through armed tensions."

"You're a philosopher," Frank replied. He moved his rook in line with Ziggy's king. "Check."

"That's an improper move!" Ziggy protested. "You are supposed to take the queen."

"So sue me," Frank said calmly.

"You would think that someone with Frank's brains would act more mature when playing such a sophisticated game," Joe said.

They all looked at Joe, surprised at his statement, except Ziggy, who kept his eyes glued to the board.

Frank was the most astonished. "Why, Joe, I didn't realize you could say a complete sentence without mentioning food, sports, or girls."

"That is a cruel thing to say," Petra protested, teasing Frank.

"Yes," Joe said with a haughty air. "He is so unrefined."

"And," Ziggy said loudly, a wide grin on his

face, "he does not know how to play chess." Ziggy moved a pawn diagonally across from Frank's king.

Frank's eyes widened to circles of astonishment. His king was trapped by Ziggy's pawn on one side, a rook on another, a knight to the side, and a bishop.

"Checkmate, you desperado!" Ziggy yelled.

Frank was shocked. "What? Not again!"

Frank and Joe's next case:

Jed Shannon, a young American movie star on location in England, has received a threat against his life. When the Hardys set out to investigate, they are drawn into a case worthy of Sherlock Holmes—and into a conspiracy as thick as the London fog.

Jillian Seabright, a beautiful British actress befriended by Jed, has vanished. The key to the mystery lies in her resemblance to missing emerald heiress Emily Cornwall. Frank and Joe trace the damsels in distress to a medieval mansion on the moors—Castle Fear. Dodging bullets and battle-axes, the boys are out to prove that chivalry is not dead—but one wrong move and they will be . . . in *Castle Fear*, Case #44 in The Hardy Boys Casefiles™.